6 - 6

The Secret
of the
Underground Room

THE SECRET
OF THE
UNDERGROUND
ROOM

JOHN BELLAIRS

Dial Books for Young Readers
New York

Published by Dial Books for Young Readers
A Division of Penguin Books USA Inc.
375 Hudson Street, New York, New York 10014

Text copyright © 1990 by John Bellairs
All rights reserved
Printed in the U.S.A.
E
First Edition
1 3 5 7 9 10 8 6 4 2

Library of Congress Cataloging in Publication Data
Bellairs, John.
Secret of the underground room / by John Bellairs
jacket by Edward Gorey.
p. cm.
Summary: When Father Higgins disappears,
Johnny Dixon and Professor Childermass discover disturbing clues
which lead them to England and an encounter with
a long-dead knight.
ISBN 0-8037-0863-7. ISBN 0-8037-0864-5 (lib. bdg.)
[1. Mystery and detective stories.
2. Knights and knighthood—Fiction.
3. England—Fiction.]
I. Title.
PZ7.B413Se 1990 [Fic]—dc20 90-3152 CIP AC

*To Lyla, a good friend
in a difficult time*

The Secret
of the
Underground Room

CHAPTER ONE

"But is he ever going to come back, professor?" asked Johnny. "Will they let him?"

Professor Childermass shrugged. "I hope so," he said glumly. "But it's his bishop's decision. Father Higgins is a priest, and he has to go wherever the church sends him. Johnny, would you hand me my nine iron? I'm going to have to chip onto the green."

It was a chilly May morning in the early nineteen fifties. Professor Childermass and his young friend Johnny Dixon were out on the Duston Heights golf course. The professor was hacking away furiously at the ball and was not doing very well. He was a short, cranky-looking man with wild, white hair, in his early seventies. His nose looked like an overripe strawberry, and on it a pair of gold-rimmed spectacles was perched crookedly. Though he had a rotten temper, the professor was really very kind underneath. Johnny Dixon, who was short and blond and shy and about thirteen years old, also wore glasses. Today he was lugging a heavy, old leather bag full of golf clubs. Johnny didn't play golf, but he enjoyed the professor's company, so he had volunteered to come along and be his caddy for the morning. As they walked around the course, Johnny and the professor talked about the problems that Father Higgins had been having lately.

Father Thomas Higgins was a friend of Johnny and the professor too. Until recently he had been the pastor of St. Michael's Catholic church in Duston Heights, a town in eastern Massachusetts. But in March Father Higgins had gotten transferred to Rocks Village, a tiny town on the Merrimack River. He was now the pastor of Holy Angels church, which had a congregation of only about two dozen people. The professor said that Father Higgins was miserable—he felt that the people in Rocks Village didn't like him. But the professor and Johnny knew Father Higgins was the kindest and gentlest of men, and they cared for him a lot. They both missed his friendship and guitar playing, as well as his delightful stories. If they could have waved a magic wand and brought him back to St. Michael's church, they would have. But they couldn't. They could only talk and worry and wonder how he was.

As Johnny watched, the professor lunged awkwardly

at the ball. He hit it high into the air and it landed on the green, but instead of staying there, it rolled off the far edge and landed in a sand trap. For a moment the professor glared at the empty green. Then he sighed, dug his hand into his pants pocket, and pulled out another ball. With a flick of his hand he spun the ball onto the green, and it rolled a few feet from the cup.

"Everyone's entitled to a little cheating now and then," he muttered as they walked toward the green. "Otherwise one might smash his clubs into kindling wood and then have to buy a new set."

Johnny smiled wanly and nodded as the professor stepped up to the ball and began lining up his putt. In the middle of his fussing, the old man looked up suddenly. "By the way," he said slyly, "did Higgy tell you that he thinks there's a ghost in the house he's living in?"

Johnny's mouth dropped open. "No," he said in a stunned voice. "I talked to him on the phone the other day, but he didn't say anything about that."

The professor picked up the golf ball and studied it. "He probably didn't want to frighten you," he added thoughtfully. "It's an odd story, and I really don't know what to make of it, but . . . well, I think the whole thing ought to be looked into." After a short pause the professor went into a pitcher's windup and heaved the golf ball into a distant clump of bushes. "Come on," he said, grabbing Johnny by the arm. "I've had enough of this idiotic game! I'll buy you a bottle of soda at the clubhouse, and then we can talk some more. How does that sound?"

With a relieved sigh, Johnny said that it sounded fine.

At the clubhouse Johnny guzzled orange soda while the professor talked about the ghost Father Higgins had seen one night. It was a young girl, and she was walking along one of the side aisles of the church. She started up the steps to the organ loft, but then she vanished. Father Higgins claimed he felt her presence at other times both in the church and at home. And he began to get odd notes scrawled on old yellowed scraps of paper.

Johnny put down his soda bottle and stared at the professor. "Notes? Do you mean they came in the mail?"

The professor shook his head impatiently. "No, no, no! I don't mean that at all! He found the notes tacked to doorposts and lying on his desk or on his bureau. One of them was stuck into his big red missal, the book he reads the Mass prayers from. They were all written in Palmer-method handwriting, which is a very fancy style that is often taught in Catholic schools."

Johnny hunched forward in his seat. "What did the notes say?"

The professor shook his head. "Oh, all sorts of silly things. One of them said *Half a moon is bad—a full moon might be worse—or is it?* Make something of that if you can! Another one said *Remember the funeral of King Charles the First.* None of the notes seemed to have any connection with any of the others, and yet Father Higgins seems to think they're important. He's saved them all, believe it or not."

Johnny frowned and took a sip of soda. "Do *you* think the notes mean anything, professor?" he asked. "I mean, could they be part of a riddle or something like that?"

The professor laughed. "Riddle diddle!" he said scornfully. "If you want to know what I think, there's some practical joker on the loose, and he is trying to make life miserable for poor old Higgy! As for that ghost, I think she was conjured up by loneliness and the heebie-jeebies. You know what a nervous man Higgy is, don't you? And he's really unhappy about his new job. I think he's seeing things that aren't there. It really bothers me." The professor frowned and bit his lip. "I worry about him a lot these days," he went on, "and I wish there were a way to get him back here to St. Michael's, where he belongs. But I can't do that, sooo . . ."

The professor paused and lit a cigarette. Johnny always hated it when the professor left him hanging. "So what are you going to do?" asked Johnny at last.

"I'm going to visit him," the professor said calmly. "It's not as if he lived on the dark side of the moon— he's only about ten miles away. I would have gone long before this, but I had the feeling that he didn't want company. At any rate, that was the impression I got from talking to him on the phone. Lately, however, he has seemed more open, so I'm going to charge on out there. I want to find out how he is, and I want to see if

I can make any sense of this blithering nonsense about notes and ghosts. Would you care to come with me?"

Johnny nodded eagerly, and so it was decided. Next Saturday they would drive down to Rocks Village and try to cheer up Father Higgins.

It was a drizzly, chilly evening as they arrived in Rocks Village, a tiny cluster of picturesque eighteenth-century houses near a seventy-year-old iron bridge. Next to the small white church stood an ugly old stone house with a rotting wooden porch. This was where Father Higgins lived. As he and the professor trotted up the mossy sidewalk, Johnny felt sorry for Father Higgins, who had to live in this damp and desolate place. They mounted the steps, and the professor pushed the doorbell button. Soon the oak door swung open, and there stood Father Higgins. He was big and burly, with a grizzled, square jaw and bushy eyebrows. Father Higgins was wearing his black clerical outfit, but he had taken off the stiff white collar. To Johnny he looked pale and worn, and there were dark circles under his eyes. But when he saw his friends, Father Higgins smiled broadly and stepped out onto the porch to shake hands with them.

"It's great to see you two!" he boomed happily. "Great and fine and terrific! Come on in and make yourselves comfortable."

The professor and Johnny followed Father Higgins down a dark hallway and into the study. It was a cozy, old-fashioned room, with dark woodwork and bookcases built into the walls. A bright fire burned in the brick fireplace, and the firelight danced over two brown leather-covered armchairs and Father Higgins's huge mahogany desk. Two bronze floor lamps lit the room—they looked as if they would be hard to lift.

"Well, here we all are!" said Father Higgins a bit nervously. He walked to the mantel and took down a cut-glass decanter. Carefully he poured two glasses of sherry, for the professor and himself, and then he went out to the kitchen. He came back with a bottle of Coke for Johnny and a tall glass full of ice. When they were all settled, Father Higgins sipped his sherry and gazed thoughtfully into the fire. He seemed to be waiting for somebody to speak.

"Have you had any more problems with this . . . uh . . . ghost business?" asked the professor at last.

Father Higgins gave his friend a look. "I know what you think, Rod," he growled. "You think I need a psychiatrist or a long rest. Well, *I* don't believe that I'm seeing things—I really, truly don't. The other night I woke up to find the girl standing by my bed!"

"Oh my gosh!" exclaimed Johnny, clapping his hands to his face. "Father, what did you do?"

Father Higgins grimaced and picked up an empty briar pipe that lay on his smoking stand. He toyed with it as he talked.

"I was never so frightened in all my life," he said slowly, "but somehow I managed to control myself. Then I remembered the old legend that ghosts sometimes want to tell you or show you something. Sure enough, the girl seemed to be motioning to me as she backed away toward the door. So I got up and followed. She led me out the front door of the house and down a path that takes you to the side door of the church. It was a dark, moonless night, but somehow I was able to see the girl— a gray glow hovered about her. She climbed the steps to the organ loft. There's nothing up there but an old broken pipe organ and some folding chairs and a lot of dust and cobwebs. The girl motioned toward the dark space behind the organ, and she smiled strangely. Then she vanished."

The professor sat staring at Father Higgins with his mouth open. "Well?" he said irritably. "You're not going to keep us in suspense, are you? Surely there's more to your story."

Father Higgins gave his friend an odd look. "I wish it all had ended there—I really do. But as it happens, I found something lying in the dust behind the organ. It was a small, flat package wrapped in brown paper and tied with twine. The twine was rotting, and from the layer of dust on the package, it looked as if it had been lying there for a long time. A very long time. At any rate, I picked the thing up and took it back to my study. Would you care to see what I found?"

The professor glowered at Father Higgins. "Show us, Higgy, or I'll poison your sherry and let the air out of the tires on your car."

Normally Father Higgins would have laughed at a

remark like this. But instead he just nodded and got up from his chair. Crossing to his desk, he took a key from his pocket and unlocked the wide, shallow drawer in the middle. Johnny and the professor got up and crowded in next to the priest, one on either side. After a brief pause Father Higgins reached into the drawer and pulled out something that looked like half of a broken green glass plate. Embedded in the glass were four little golden fish, which seemed to be swimming in a green sea. A dirty index card was held to the glass with a piece of red sealing wax, and on it these words were neatly printed:

To raise the dead.

CHAPTER TWO

In silence Johnny and the two men stared at the broken piece of green glass. For quite a while no one could think of anything to say, but finally the professor harrumphed self-importantly.

"Humph. Humph. God's teeth, Higgy! Is *this* the prize in the cereal box? It reminds me of a salad plate my Aunt Sally used to own—or rather, I should say, it reminds me of half a salad plate. Where's the rest of it?"

Father Higgins shrugged. "Search me. This was all I found. But you know, Roderick, I don't think this is a salad plate or anything so ordinary. The glass is heavy, and . . . well, somehow it seems old. I'll bet it's a piece of stained glass from an old cathedral. Whatever it is, I haven't had a good night's sleep since I found the thing. I keep dreaming that my mother has come to visit me, and that we're sitting up late at night here in the study, talking." Father Higgins sighed. "As you know, Roderick, my mother died several years ago. But I still keep dreaming that she's here. Maybe it's because there are a lot of things I wish I had said to her when she was alive. But I'm getting off the subject: Every night when I've had this dream, I wake up standing here in the study, in the dark. And I have the piece of glass in my hands!"

Johnny gasped. "Wow, Father, that is weird!" He added hesitantly, "Do . . . do you sleepwalk a lot?"

Father Higgins shook his head. "No. In fact I've never been a sleepwalker in my entire life—until now. Some piece of devilry is going on, and I'd love to know why!" Frowning, the priest slid the piece of glass back into the drawer and locked it. He pocketed the key and turned to the professor with a questioning look. "Do you think I'm going nuts, Rod?" he asked. "Come on—be honest with me."

The professor took a Balkan Sobranie cigarette from the box in his pocket and lit one. "I'd say you were the victim of some kind of obsession. You found that glass with the note on it, and then you started thinking about your mother. You were quarreling with her at the time she died, weren't you?"

Father Higgins nodded sadly. "Yes. She didn't want me to be a priest—she wanted me to be a lawyer instead. All right, so I might have had my mother on my mind when I found the piece of glass. But how do you explain the ghost leading me to it?"

The professor smiled patiently. "Higgy, you know as well as I do that people sometimes see things that aren't there. You may have seen a shaft of moonlight, and then your imagination did the rest."

Father Higgins glowered, and the back of his neck started to get red. He poked a hairy finger into the professor's face. "You pompous old crumdum!" he thundered. "Are you telling me that I was scared by a patch of moonlight? Is that what you're trying to say?"

The professor stepped back and looked quickly away. He and Father Higgins were old friends, and he didn't want to start a fight. "Well, uh, Higgy, I didn't exactly say that. What I meant was, er, well . . ."

Still frowning, Father Higgins walked quickly back to the desk and jerked open a side drawer. He reached in and pulled out a handful of yellowed slips of paper. With a flourish he spread them out on top of the desk. "All right, you great genius!" he grumbled. "Have a look at these and tell me if they look like moonlight!"

Johnny glanced nervously from the professor to Father Higgins. He had the awful feeling that the two of them were going to get into an argument, right in front of his eyes. And so he was very relieved when the professor burst out laughing. He pulled his handkerchief out of his pocket and waved it in the air as a signal of surrender.

"All right, I give up!" he exclaimed, still chuckling. "Higgy, you're the only person in the world who is more cranky and grouchy than I am, but I like you anyway. Let's see these notes that you told me about over the phone."

Johnny and the professor walked to the desk and stooped to examine the mysterious messages. As Father Higgins had said, they were all written in a fancy, flowery handwriting, full of loops and swirls. This is what they said:

The church of the faceless images.
Half a moon is bad—a full moon might be worse—or is it?
Remember the funeral of King Charles the First.
Son of man, shall these bones live?
Drake cake. Bustard custard. Go on. . . .
When Vega is high in the sky.
They must both be destroyed.
You may be wrong about everything.

After squinting owlishly at each note, the professor piled them in a neat little stack in the middle of the desk. Then he folded his arms, heaved a weary sigh, and turned to Father Higgins. "Higgy," he said, slowly, "has it ever occurred to you that you might be the victim of some lunatic practical joker? I mean, you told me that there were people out here who didn't like you very much. Well, isn't it possible that one of them left these nitwitted notes for you?"

Father Higgins folded his arms and looked grumpy.

"Ye-es," he said slowly, "I suppose it's possible. All sorts of things are possible. There might be green men on Mars with tennis rackets for hands. There might be hockey players skating on the rings of Saturn. But I'll tell you this, Roderick: I've seen what I've seen, and I'm pretty sure that there are dark and supernatural forces at work in this house and in the church next door. And if you doubt what I say . . . well, someday you may be very sorry."

The professor flinched, as if Father Higgins had just slapped him in the face. What if his friend was right? If the professor made fun of his fears, and then found out too late that Father Higgins really was in danger . . .

"I apologize," sighed the professor as he gave his friend a reassuring pat on the arm. "You have good reason to be annoyed with me, Higgy. I guess I'm just trying to make up clever explanations for things that frighten me. Those notes are mysterious, but there's also something sinister about them—all that talk of funerals and bones and then the card that says *To raise the dead*. What do *you* think it all means, my friend?"

Father Higgins shrugged. "You've got me. As I said, I feel that devilry is afoot, but I don't know what form it will take. That's what's so scary—I don't know what direction the punch will be coming from."

"Maybe you should move back to Duston Heights," said Johnny hopefully.

Father Higgins bit his lip. "I can't. And if I tell Bishop Monohan about all this, he'll think I'm ready for the loony bin." Father Higgins set his jaw and looked grim. "No," he said in a determined voice. "I'm just going to have to wait and see what happens. Maybe nothing will— maybe we're all getting frightened for no reason. But in any case, if I could face the jungles of the Philippines during World War Two, I guess I can face ghosts and notes and old pieces of glass."

The professor eyed his friend skeptically. "Perhaps," he said. "But if I were you, I'd get some doctor to pre- scribe sleeping pills. You look like you've been dragged around for miles. And I think we should change the subject now and talk about something cheerful. John and I have to be going pretty soon, and we haven't seen you in a long time. It'd be a shame to spend our whole visit jabbering about evil things. The way we're going, we'll be giving John nightmares."

"I'm not scared," muttered Johnny defiantly. He fol- lowed the two men back to the easy chairs, and they chattered pleasantly for a while about baseball, Ted Williams's batting average, and the rickety aerial that the professor had built on his roof so he could listen to the Red Sox games. Finally the professor pulled out his pocket watch and announced that it was time to leave. Father Higgins looked sad, and it was clear that he wanted them to stay longer. But he led his friends to the door and shook their hands vigorously.

"Thanks for coming, both of you," he said with a warm smile. "It's good to know I'm not alone in the world."

"You most certainly are not!" said the professor with a mischievous grin. "After all, who else do I know who plays such a bad game of chess? Play the way you did the last time I saw you, and you'll always have at least one friend."

The two men laughed, and they all said their good-byes. As they trotted down the walk toward the car, Johnny gave the professor a worried glance.

"He doesn't look good, does he?" whispered Johnny.

The professor shook his head sadly. "No. Not good at all. I wish he would try to get the bishop to give him two months off and an airplane ticket to the Bahamas. But Higgy is at least as stubborn as I am, and you know how bad *that* is. I just hope he knows what he's doing."

As he got into the car, Johnny looked back toward the house. Father Higgins still stood in the lighted doorway. He raised his hand and waved weakly. Johnny felt a pang of fear for his friend. Would he be all right out here?

Weeks passed, and as the school year wound down toward its end, Johnny became involved in a lot of activities: He got a part in the Latin Club's play, which was a shortened version of Shakespeare's *Julius Caesar*. He took piano lessons so he could do well in the June recital, and he played in chess tournaments with schools in nearby towns. But while all this was going on, he kept thinking about Father Higgins.

One Friday evening early in June, Johnny was sitting in the kitchen with his grandfather. Johnny lived with his grandparents, because his mother was dead and his father was flying a jet in the Air Force. Their home was a big white house across the street from the professor's stucco mansion, and it was full of homey, comfortable, old-fashioned furniture. The kitchen table was round and made of oak, with ball-and-claw feet. Johnny was drinking a Coke and talking about a movie that he and his friend Fergie had seen a few hours earlier. Grampa Dixon, who was standing by the stove warming some milk in a pan, was a tall, stoop-shouldered man with a few gray hairs strung across the freckled dome of his head. The flesh of his face was loose and wrinkly, and his eyes twinkled behind gold-rimmed spectacles.

"Do you like pirate movies?" asked Grampa as he poured the milk into a glass. "I remember once I saw Doug Fairbanks in . . . lemme see, what was the name of it? *The Sea Hawk*, I guess. That was an old silent film, but it was still pretty good. Y'see, in those days— *Hey, wouldja look at that!*"

Suddenly Johnny whirled around. Grampa had rushed to the kitchen window, and he was peering anxiously out into the night. After a few seconds he stepped back, took off his glasses, and rubbed his eyes.

"I must be seein' things," he mumbled as he put his glasses back on. "Darnedest thing, though. It looked like he was there!"

Johnny was totally confused and alarmed. "Who, Grampa? Who did you see?"

Grampa turned to Johnny with a wondering frown on his face. "Well, while I was talkin' to you a minute ago," he began slowly, "I sorta glanced out the window, an' I thought I saw Father Higgins standin' out there under the streetlight, an' . . ."

Johnny's mouth dropped open. *"Father Higgins?* What would he be doing out there?"

Grampa shrugged. "Search me! It sure looked like it was him, though. Well, by the time I got to the window to have a closer look, he was gone! Can you beat that?"

Johnny felt queasy inside. His grandfather was not the kind of person who imagined things, and when he was wearing his glasses, his eyesight was pretty good. "I'll run outside and have a look," said Johnny nervously.

"Yeah, you do that," said Grampa. "If it is him, ask him why he doesn't come in an' see us."

Fearfully, Johnny opened the screen door and stepped out into the backyard. It was a warm night, and lightning bugs were winking under the chestnut tree that grew at the far end of the yard. Johnny padded across the wet grass, around the side of the house, and out onto the sidewalk. Lights were on in most of the houses on Fillmore Street, but no one was out walking. The old-fashioned streetlamp glowed as Johnny glanced anxiously around. He peered into the dark mass of evergreen bushes that grew in front of the house next door. "F-father?" he said timidly. Then, cupping his hands to his mouth, he called out more loudly. "Father Higgins? Are you there?"

Dead silence. In the distance a door slammed, but that was all.

With a troubled expression on his face Johnny walked back to the house. As he stepped into the kitchen, he saw Grampa sitting at the table sipping his warm milk. The old man looked up. "Johnny? Didja find . . ."

Johnny shook his head. "Nope. Nobody. And it's kind of hard to believe that Father Higgins is playing hide-and-seek with us."

Grampa gave Johnny a sheepish look. "Y'mean you think I imagined it?"

Tears sprang to Johnny's eyes, and he rushed to his grandfather's side. "Oh, no, Grampa! I didn't mean anything like that, honest I didn't! Only it's all just . . . well, kinda strange."

Grampa rubbed his chin thoughtfully. "Yeah," he said. "It sure is." There was a long pause as the two of them just looked at each other. Then, wearily, the old man shoved his chair back and dragged himself to his feet. "Well, g'night, Johnny," he said as he started for the door. "Sleep tight."

Johnny stood watching as his grandfather left the room. Cold fear clutched at his heart. He could not explain what his grandfather had seen, and it scared him. With a puzzled look on his face, Johnny turned out the kitchen lights, went upstairs, and began taking off his clothes. After he had changed into his pajamas and brushed his teeth, he sat down on his bed and watched the long linen curtains sway in the night breeze that blew in through the open window. His feeling of uneasiness had not gone away—it had gotten worse. But he was also tired and very much wanted to go to sleep. He looked around at the scarred bureau and tall walnut clothes closet that stood in the corner. It was a nice room to be in, even when you weren't feeling particularly good. Johnny walked over to the door and turned out the overhead light. Then he pulled back the top sheet and climbed into bed.

Aaah. It felt great to be tucked in between cool, sweet-smelling sheets. Gramma kept cedar nuts in all the bureau drawers, and the wonderful smell of them filled Johnny's nostrils. His nervousness had died, and sleep was stealing over him. But after he had drifted off, he found that he was having a very unpleasant dream. He dreamed he was still asleep in bed, but somehow he was able to see the moonlit room clearly. He heard a sound. A ghostly knocking was coming from the clothes closet. At first it was faint, but gradually it grew louder, and then the paneled doors started to shake, and the curved brass handles moved up and down. Still dreaming, Johnny felt his fear mount until it became blind panic, and at that moment he woke with a start. The peaceful room lay in darkness, except for one long gray slash of moonlight across the carpeted floor. Then Johnny turned to his left, and he saw a tall, hulking, shadowy man sitting in the chair next to his bed. The figure looked like Father Higgins.

CHAPTER THREE

Johnny was too scared to scream. He sat bolt upright in bed, rigid with terror. His mouth was open, and his jaw trembled. Many minutes passed before he was able to turn his head and stare directly at the fearful shape— but it was gone. In its place, on the seat of the cane-bottomed chair, lay something shiny. Quickly Johnny lurched to his right and clicked on the lamp that stood on his bedside table. Then he fumbled for his glasses and put them on. He turned back to the chair. And what was lying there? A teaspoon. The handle was shaped like a bearded man in a long robe, and under the man's feet was a tiny pedestal labeled THOMAS. Tied to an ornamental loop at the top of the spoon was a price tag. But the price on the tag had been crossed out, and instead these groups of letters had been scrawled on the cardboard:

Sn   Cu   Sb

Johnny's head was whirling. He still had not gotten over his fright, and now he had to puzzle over this object that had been left on his chair. What did it all mean? Was Father Higgins dead? Johnny read a lot, and he had heard stories of how ghosts of living people sometimes appeared to their friends, to warn them or to ask for help. To ask for help. Johnny's head was beginning to clear, and this seemed to be the most likely explanation for what he had just seen. The last time he had talked to Father Higgins, the poor man had been up to his ears in trouble. But if he was asking for help, what kind of help did he need?

Johnny sat on the edge of his bed for a long while, turning the funny little spoon over and over in his hands. Then sleepiness came over him, and he felt his eyelids beginning to flutter. With a sigh he laid the spoon back on the chair, took off his glasses, and snapped off the light. In the morning he would talk to the professor, and together they would figure the mystery out. Johnny laid his head on the pillow and slid off into deep, delicious sleep.

The next day was Saturday. Usually on Saturdays Johnny had a long leisurely breakfast of pancakes and sausages prepared by Gramma. But today he wanted to skip breakfast altogether and tear over to the professor's house to tell him about the things he had seen last night. Unfortunately, he couldn't do this. Gramma would have been disappointed. So Johnny fought down his impatience and munched pancakes and tried to chat pleasantly with his grandparents. But his mind was definitely someplace else, and he wondered if either of the two old people would notice this. Grampa began telling a long story about the time he had visited Utah back in the Wild West days, when there were still gun-toting killers, tough marshals, and blue-jacketed cavalrymen roaming around. He was just getting to the exciting part when they heard a loud knocking at the front door.

"My gosh!" exclaimed Grampa as he got up. "I wonder who *that* is. Sounds like he's tryin' to break down the door!"

"Whoever it is, he doesn't have the brains to use the doorbell," Gramma said. Calmly she flipped a pancake on the griddle. "You'd think people would notice where the button is," she added.

Walking slowly because of his arthritis, Grampa went to the door. When he opened it, there stood the professor, looking more disheveled than usual. His glasses were stuck crookedly on his face, and his hair was a mess. He was still wearing his pajama top, which was tucked clumsily into his trousers. His face was red, and he was breathing hard.

"Henry!" he gasped, stumbling into the front hall. "It's . . . there's never been a . . . I mean, how . . ." After giving Grampa a very wild, confused glance, the professor brushed past him and headed straight for the kitchen. When he got there, he stopped in the middle of the floor and just stood still, breathing heavily and looking from Johnny to Gramma and back to Johnny again. Johnny was alarmed, and he jumped up from his seat.

"What . . . what is it, professor?" he exclaimed.

The professor closed his eyes, and with a struggle he pulled himself together and slumped into a chair, folding his hands on the kitchen table. Staring hard at the sugar bowl, he began to talk in a quiet, matter-of-fact voice.

"Father Higgins has disappeared," he said. "I just got a call from his housekeeper. He didn't show up to say Mass this morning, so people got worried, and they went over to his house, and it was totally empty. No Father Higgins, no Father Higgins anywhere. Search parties are out looking for him in the woods near Rocks Village and . . . and . . ." Here the professor paused and choked back a sob. ". . . And they are even dragging the river."

Johnny turned pale and swallowed hard. Had he seen the ghost of the dead Father Higgins? Or had he seen something else? More than ever, he wanted to be in some private place so he could talk with the professor. Gramma and Grampa were nice people, but they didn't believe much in ghosts and specters and things that go bump in the night.

Gramma clucked and said sympathetic things, and Grampa asked a lot of questions that the professor couldn't answer. Then silence fell. The kitchen clock buzzed, and you could hear children playing at the end of the street.

"I wish I could think of something to do," said the professor in a dull, despairing voice. "But I can't. We'll just have to wait and see if the poor man shows up. I have a full load of classes and meetings today, but I'll go down to the church and say a prayer for him tonight."

"Can I go down with you?" said Johnny suddenly.

The professor turned and stared curiously at his young friend. The two of them knew each other very well, and sometimes one would know what the other was thinking without a word being spoken. Instantly the professor guessed that Johnny had something important to tell him, something that he couldn't talk about in front of his grandparents.

"Why . . . why yes, John, of course you may go down to the church with me," said the professor in a stiff, formal voice. "I . . . hrumph! . . . don't always believe that lighting candles and praying will solve things, but I don't suppose it'll hurt any. Shall we say eight o'clock?"

That evening Johnny and the professor were sitting in one of the front pews at St. Michael's church. The smell of incense still hung in the air from an earlier service. As clearly as he could, Johnny told the old man about what he had seen last night. The professor listened intently, and he nodded gravely or shook his head every now and then. When he had finished his tale,

Johnny reached into his pocket and pulled out the spoon. Without a word, he handed it to the professor.

Thoughtfully, the professor turned the shiny object over in his hands. After what seemed like a long time, he spoke.

"So this is what he left?" he asked.

Johnny nodded. "Yeah. Professor, what do you think it means?"

The professor rubbed his chin thoughtfully. "Well, to begin with," he said, slowly, "this is what they call an apostle spoon. People used to buy them in sets and hang them in wooden racks on their dining room walls. Each of the twelve spoons had a handle that looked like one of the twelve apostles who followed Jesus. This one is Thomas—as it should be, since that is Father Higgins's first name."

"What about the tag, professor?" asked Johnny. "What do those letters mean?"

The professor smiled faintly. "You know," he began, "it's funny what you remember from high school chemistry. Those are symbols for three elements: *Sn* stands for tin, *Cu* copper, and *Sb* antimony. They're all metals. Beyond that, I don't have the faintest idea why Higgy would have given you that spoon with that tag on it."

There was a long silence. Johnny stared at the red sanctuary lamp that cast weird shadows across the church's altar. "Do . . . do you think he's alive?" he asked in a weak, throaty voice. "Father Higgins, I mean."

The professor twiddled the spoon back and forth between his fingers. "Yes," he said firmly, "I honestly do. You were right when you said that ghosts of the living sometimes appear to people. And when you think about it, why would Higgy appear to you and leave mysterious messages if he were dead? No one could help him then. So I think we have to believe that he's trying to contact us. But I don't know if there's anything we can do—we just don't have enough to go on. I'm going to call up a friend of mine tonight. He's a chemistry prof at Haggstrum College, and he might know if there's any connection between the three metals that are listed on that tag. And now let's say a few prayers for our friend, shall we?"

Johnny nodded, and the two of them walked up to the communion rail, knelt down, and prayed for Father Higgins.

CHAPTER FOUR

Two days passed. Then one evening, as Johnny was sitting by the radio in the parlor, the phone rang. Quickly he snapped off the radio and jumped up. He ran into the front hall and picked up the receiver, and he was not terribly surprised to hear the professor's voice at the other end. He had been expecting to hear from him. However, the first thing the professor said absolutely stunned Johnny.

"Hello, John. How would you like to go to England with me?"

Johnny could not have been more surprised if the professor had invited him to go to Mars. "*England?* Professor, what's going on?"

"If you will stop yelping at me and come over here

right away, I'll tell you," said the professor smoothly. "I've just taken a pan of my fudge-covered super brownies out of the oven, and you can have some if you're good."

A few minutes later Johnny and the professor were sitting at the white-enameled table in the professor's kitchen munching brownies and drinking milk. The professor was wearing a flour-smeared white apron and a puffy white chef's hat, and every now and then Johnny would glance at the old man and see the sly, secretive smile on his face. Finally he decided that he couldn't stand the suspense any longer.

"All right, professor!" he exclaimed irritably. "You said that you were gonna take me to England. Come on, tell me about it."

The professor took another bite of his brownie and chewed it thoroughly. Then suddenly he leaned forward, put his elbows on the table, and stared intently at Johnny. "John," he said quietly, "I think I know where Higgy has gone to. You see, I took that spoon to the chemistry professor, and do you know what he told me? He said that it is made out of Britannia metal, an alloy that contains copper, tin, and antimony—the three elements whose symbols were on the tag."

Johnny stared wonderingly at the professor. "You mean . . . you think Father Higgins has gone to England?" Johnny knew that *Britannia* was one of the old names for England—he had read it somewhere.

The professor nodded gravely. "Yes," he said. "When he appeared by your bedside, that is what he was trying to tell you. You see, his mother is buried in England. And do you remember that card that was stuck onto the piece of stained glass? It said *To raise the dead.* I think that Higgy has some crazy idea that he's going to use that piece of glass to bring his mom back. Or maybe he's under some kind of evil spell that is making him do strange things. Whatever is going on, I think he needs help badly. We've got to go to England and try to find him."

England! Johnny's head was really spinning now. He had been to England once before with Fergie and the professor. It had been a sightseeing trip for the most part, but this was something different. They were going to England to save Father Higgins's life. Suddenly a thought occurred to him.

"Professor?" he said. "Do you have any idea where Father Higgins might be?"

The professor sighed. "Well," he began, slowly, "I couldn't say where he is at this moment, but I'll bet I know a town he'll be visiting: Glastonbury. It's an old rural village in the western part of England. Some people think that King Arthur and his wife were buried in the abbey there."

Johnny was getting more puzzled by the minute. "Why would Father Higgins want to go there?"

"Because that's where his mother is buried. Higgy's father was Irish and his mother was English. When her husband died, Mrs. Higgins went back to England to live with her relatives. After her death she was cremated, and her ashes were buried under the floor of a little church in Glastonbury—I remember Higgy talking about how—"

"But Catholics don't believe in cremation," said Johnny, interrupting. "How come they did that to Mrs. Higgins?"

The professor smiled. "Well, Mrs. Higgins wasn't a Catholic." The professor opened his box of cigarettes and took one out. Thoughtfully he lit it. "Of course," he said as he blew out a stream of smoke, "I could be wrong about the place Higgy has gone to—I could be wrong about a lot of things. But going to Glastonbury is better than running up and down England yelling *Higgy!* at the tops of our voices. As I said before, I really do think he wants to bring his mom back from the dead so he can talk to her. I know it sounds crazy, but a lot of crazy things have been happening to the poor man lately."

Silence. Johnny toyed with the crumbs on his plate, and then he spoke up. "Do you think my gramma and grampa will let me go?" he asked.

The professor grinned slyly. "They will if I pretend that this is an educational trip, something that will help you get better grades in school. Leave that part to me. And it's my treat, in case you were wondering. Are there any questions?"

Johnny hesitated. There was something he wanted to ask for, but he didn't know how to put it. "Professor?" he said hoarsely. "Can . . . I mean, would it be possible . . . could Fergie come with us?"   •

The professor stared for a while at the burning tip of his cigarette, and then he laughed loudly. "This is turning into an expedition, isn't it? Well—hrmph! I *suppose* we could take young Byron along. Do you think his parents would let him go?"

Johnny stared hard at the tabletop. He was beginning to feel embarrassed. "I think they would if you paid his way," he said in a low voice.

"Hmm . . ." said the professor as he scratched his chin. "You know, Byron is pretty strong, and if it turns out that Higgy is off his rocker, then it might take three of us to hold him down. All right, let's include Byron too."

Johnny was very busy for the next two weeks. He bought new clothes, read guidebooks, and talked a lot with Fergie about the trip. Finally, on a sunny, warm day, they all went down to Boston in the professor's car. The professor drove to the airport parking lot and left the car so he could use it on his return. The three of them flew across the Atlantic on a big four-engine plane, and when they landed at an airport, they took another taxi to Paddington Station in London. There they caught a train for the city of Bath, which is a double-decker-bus ride away from Glastonbury. The professor had reserved rooms for them at a Glastonbury hotel called the Cross Keys, and by the time they arrived in the evening, the travelers were very tired.

After they had been shown to their rooms, Johnny, Fergie, and the professor went down to have a cold supper in the dining room of the hotel. Then they went outdoors and walked in the mild June air. Although it was after nine-thirty, it was light enough to read a newspaper on the street. In the distance the gaunt ruins of the abbey loomed, and towering over the town rose a high steep hill called Glastonbury Tor. On top of the Tor stood a stone building called St. Michael's Tower— it looked as if it belonged to a church that had somehow mysteriously disappeared. They wandered around for only a short time and then headed back toward the inn and their nice soft beds.

The next morning, after breakfast, the professor led his two friends down the main street of the town to an old church named for St. John the Baptist. Before entering the church, the professor stepped back and peered up at the tower. Then he reached into his jacket pocket and took out a folded sheet of paper. As he opened it, the two boys crowded in next to him and peered over his shoulder. Fergie was thoroughly puzzled, but Johnny knew the professor had copied down all the mysterious notes that had been sent to Father Higgins. Smugly, the professor explained to Fergie how he had sneaked into Father Higgins's house while policemen were roaming around upstairs.

". . . and so I copied the notes down as fast as I could and scrammed," said the professor. "And I was just looking up at the tower to see if there are any faceless images on it. But there aren't." He paused and folded up the paper again. "Well, gentlemen? Shall we go in?"

The boys followed the professor into the cold, dank gloom of the old stone church. Their voices rose and echoed as they walked along, looking at the worn stones on the floor. The professor explained that this was the church where Father Higgins's mother was supposed to be buried. Many of the square flint slabs were gravestones with names and dates on them, but none mentioned Mrs. Higgins. Finally they came to a wide space in front of the high altar, where broad steps rose to a beautifully carved marble screen covered with gesturing figures. At the bottom of the steps were more inscribed stones, and the professor hunched over with his hands on his knees so he could see them better. Scuttling sideways, he went from one to the next, until suddenly he let out a loud exclamation.

"Hah!" he crowed. "This is it! My memory did not fail me after all! This is where Father Higgins's mother is buried!"

The boys moved in close to look. Sure enough, the neat letters said:

In memory of
MARY ELIZABETH HIGGINS
(1888–1946)
whose ashes repose beneath this stone

Dropping quickly to his knees, the professor examined the edges of the stone, which was cemented firmly into the pavement. There was no sign that the slab had been pried up or tampered with in any way.

"Huh!" snorted the professor as he pulled himself to his feet. "So maybe I was wrong about what Higgy is trying to do. He's had plenty of time to come here, swipe his mom's ashes, and skedaddle. But then if he isn't planning to raise his mother's—"

"Excuse me, sir," said a deep grave voice, "but I was wondering if I could be of any assistance to you?"

The professor looked up. Standing above him was a tall, lean, old clergyman in a floor-length black cassock. He had a long, horsy face and big droopy ears. A mop of white hair hung down over his forehead. Startled and flustered, the professor tried to make up a story on the spur of the moment—he didn't dare tell the man why they were really there.

"Uh . . . well, er, ahem!" spluttered the professor, as his mind raced madly. "I . . . we, that is, we have a friend in America whose mother is buried here. I promised him that we would look up his mother's grave while we were in England."

A faint smile creased the old man's lips. "How very kind of you," he said in a slightly sarcastic tone that puzzled the professor. "You are welcome to examine our church until noon, when a communion service will be held. After that . . ."

The old man rattled on, but the professor was not listening to him. He was staring into the man's eyes. Their gaze met, and the professor flinched. Quickly he glanced away, and then with a great effort the professor pulled himself together. He looked at Johnny and Fergie and forced himself to smile pleasantly at the old man. Then he coughed pompously and yanked his gold watch out of his vest pocket.

"Hem!" said the professor, popping the gold lid to read the face. "I fear that we must be off to examine the ruins of the abbey. Thank you for your kindness, sir, and I'm sorry our visit has to be so short." Awkwardly the professor started to shake hands with the clergyman, but at the last minute he closed his hand into a fist, turned, and stalked out of the church. The boys followed him with bewildered expressions on their faces. When they were outside and the church door had closed behind them, the boys turned to the professor. They were waiting for an explanation.

"What was *that* all about, prof?" asked Fergie.

The professor folded his arms and looked grim. Johnny noticed that the corner of his mouth was twitching, as it often did when he was upset. "I'll explain it to you in a minute," said the professor in a strained voice. "I just don't want to talk about it now. What a shock! Let's go and have a look at the ruins of the abbey."

A few minutes later they were walking among the tall, roofless stone walls of Glastonbury Abbey. Normally the professor would have been talking a mile a minute, but he was dead silent. They wandered across the well-trimmed grass till they came to a low brick wall that lay beyond the great towering masses of wrecked stone. The professor sat down on the wall and took out a black cardboard box decorated with a gold two-headed eagle. From it he plucked a black-and-gold cigarette, and when it was lit, he stared off into space with the strangest of looks on his face. By now the boys were very impatient—the professor obviously knew something, and they wanted to know it too.

"Come on, professor!" said Johnny anxiously. "If you've found out anything, we have a right to know too!"

"Yeah," chimed in Fergie.

The professor's face was stony. He went on smoking awhile before he spoke. "When I was talking to that old clergyman," he began, slowly, "I happened to look into his eyes, and if I had a weak heart I probably wouldn't be talking to you now. Boys, I tell you—that old man has *Father Higgins's eyes!*"

Johnny gasped. "Are you sure?"

The professor nodded. "Higgy's eyes are a peculiar shade of green, with little yellow flecks mixed in. I know him well enough to say that those are his eyes. There is absolutely no doubt about it in my mind. A lot of people never notice the special things about a person's appearance, but I always do!"

The boys looked at each other. They knew the professor well, and he wasn't acting any crazier than he usually did. Could he be right? And if so, what did all this mean?

Fergie gave the professor a skeptical glance. "So do you mean that Father Higgins is dead, and that old coot stole his eyes?"

"No, no, *no!*" snapped the professor. "I didn't say that at all! What I mean is that that was Father Higgins we were talking to. Some evil spirit has invaded his body, and it has changed his appearance for some unknown reason. And if you ask me why some spirit would want to snatch our poor friend, I don't know! Lord above! Not in my wildest dreams would I have believed that this was possible!"

CHAPTER FIVE

For a long time the three of them sat there watching the other tourists prowl among the ruins. The morning sun cast long shadows on the grass, and birds twittered in the thorn tree nearby. Johnny could hardly believe that what the professor was saying really was true. But if it was, what chance did they have of finding Father Higgins? If some evil force was strong enough to change the priest's appearance, what could the three of them do?

As if in answer to Johnny's thoughts, the professor spoke. "I don't think we ought to give up," he said with tight-jawed determination. "At least we know that Higgy is here, and we have to wait for him to make his move. Why he hasn't swiped his mother's ashes already, who knows? Maybe the evil spirit doesn't want what Higgy wants, and is fighting against his will. Maybe there's a night watchman in the church, or an electric-eye system or something like that. But I'm sure he wants his mother's ashes, or he wouldn't be here."

Fergie looked exasperated. "So what are we supposed to do?" he asked. "Camp outside the church door and wait for this old white-haired character to show up?"

"No," said the professor calmly. "That would be kind of silly, wouldn't it? The clergyman would spot us. No, I think we should just let Father Higgins dig the ashes up and then try to follow him. That shouldn't be too hard because there are only two ways he can get out of town—by bus or by car. People visiting from out of town have to leave their car license numbers at the hotels they're staying at, and there are only two hotels in town, ours and the Royal George down the street. I've checked out the local license plates and I know the numbers they start with. There are no out-of-town plates listed in the register at our hotel, and I've already checked the Royal George, just to see if Higgy was traveling under a fake name. No out-of-town plates there either. So, that leaves the bus station. We'll check it, and hopefully there will be someone around who remembers a horsy-faced British clergyman and where he was bound for."

"But where do you think he'll be going to?" asked Johnny.

The professor shrugged. "That's something we'll find

out later. If I'm right, he has to work some magic ritual to bring his mother back from the dead. And the ritual probably has something to do with that piece of green glass that he showed us. The day I invaded his house and copied his notes, I looked in the desk drawer where he kept the glass—the drawer was unlocked, and the glass was gone. So he must have it with him. Remember what one of the notes said? *Half a moon is bad—a full moon might be worse—or is it?* If you want to be imaginative, a round piece of glass could be like the moon. Well, I will bet that there is another piece of glass out there, the other half of this 'moon' that the note is talking about. Somehow, Higgy has got to get his hands on it, and that is why we're going to follow him."

As he listened to this speech, Fergie got more and more irritated. "Prof!" he exclaimed in exasperation. "How are we gonna follow Father Higgins around if he keeps changing his shape?"

The professor sighed and took a long drag on his cigarette. "I was afraid you'd say something like that, Byron," he growled. "You've got a good point—I can't deny it. But when you don't have much to go on, you have to gamble." The professor held up two knobby fingers. "I'm betting on two things," he said. "First, that the spirit that has possessed Higgy doesn't realize yet that we're onto him. Second, that he will go on making Higgy look like an elderly English clergyman. There are reasons why he might do this. Old clergymen are terribly respectable, and they aren't likely to be challenged by cops or anyone else." The professor looked sharply from one boy to the other. "Gentlemen," he said, "I realize that I'm betting on a thousand-to-one shot. But there's not much else that we can do, is there?"

The professor and the boys whiled away the day as well as they could. They took a Green Line bus to the nearby town of Wells and wandered through the famous old cathedral. They admired the astronomical clock and the other treasures that the church held, and they fed the swans that swim in the moat that surrounds the bishop's palace. They drank tea and munched cream cakes covered with strawberry jam in a small old-fashioned tea shop. By the time they got back to Glastonbury, it was five in the evening. As soon as they got off the bus, they went back to the church of St. John to see if Mrs. Higgins's tomb slab had been moved. It had not, so they went to look at the abbey once more and then returned to their hotel to have dinner. By now they were all thoroughly exhausted, and they spent the evening reading and writing letters in the hotel lounge.

Next morning, when the professor and the boys gathered in the dining room for breakfast, they noticed immediately that something was going on. Waiters and maids and hotel residents were standing around in groups and talking excitedly to each other. Immediately the professor guessed what had happened. Putting on his best no-nonsense manner, he strode up to one group and coughed loudly.

"Hem! Excuse me, folks, but is . . . is something the matter?"

One waiter turned to him and smiled sourly. "You might say so, sir. It seems that someone broke into St. John's church last night around midnight and knocked the watchman cold. Then he pried up a stone in the floor and made off with the ashes of a lady who was buried there. As you might imagine, there's been quite a commotion."

The professor pretended to be surprised. "Good heavens!" he exclaimed. "Why on earth would anyone do such a thing?"

The waiter shrugged. "I can't imagine, sir. This is a very quiet town usually, and that's why everyone is so upset."

The professor nodded stiffly to the waiter and went back to the table, where the boys were waiting. When he told them the news, they felt relieved. At last it had happened.

Fergie stared hard at the professor. "Okay, prof," he said. "So what do we do now?"

The professor sipped his coffee. "We finish our breakfasts and check out of the hotel. Then we go down to the bus station to see if an elderly, white-haired clergyman has left on a bus at any time this morning."

"What if he left last night?" asked Johnny anxiously.

"He couldn't have," said the professor with a confident smile. "The break-in happened around midnight, and British bus stations don't stay open that late in these small towns. No. He'll probably leave this morning, and I don't mind if he gets a head start on us—I just want to know where the devil he's going!"

About an hour later the three travelers showed up at the Glastonbury bus station with suitcases in hand. Big green double-decker buses were pulled up under a long porch, and behind the porch was a ticket office. When the professor asked the ticket seller about the old clergyman, the man's eyes lit up immediately.

"Strange you should mention it, sir," he said with a puzzled frown. "Strange indeed. Early this morning I sold a ticket to an elderly clerical chap who looked like the one you described. And I must say, he acted *very* odd! Kept looking around as if somebody was after him. Made me nervous just to talk to him, and I was glad when he left."

The professor swallowed hard and tried to act calm. "Did . . . did the man say where he was going?"

The clerk smiled "Well, sir," he said, "my memory isn't that good, but he paid with a travelers' check, and it ought to be in this drawer here. A moment please."

As the professor fiddled impatiently with his watch chain, the ticket seller dug through a collection of papers in the drawer below his desk. It seemed to take forever.

"Ah!" he said at last. "Here it is. A check from the Reverend Dr. Rufus Masterman. And he bought a ticket to Bristol." The man paused and glanced uncertainly at the professor. "Are you with the police or the American FBI, sir?"

The professor laughed loudly and shook his head. "Oh, no! I . . . well, this old man is a relative of mine, and he's been acting a bit peculiar lately. Thank you for your information. I think the boys and I had better go to Bristol and find out what dear old Dr. Masterman is up to."

A bus for Bristol arrived twenty minutes later, and the professor and the boys got aboard. Bristol is a port city on the west coast of England, near the Bristol Channel. Huge hills loom over the center of the city, where canals have been dug from the nearby river Avon. The canals are called the Floating Harbor, and ships from all over the world dock there. The professor got rooms for himself and the boys at the Grand Hotel, a very dignified old establishment on Broad Street. He couldn't afford to stay long at this place, but he felt that the boys ought to have the experience of staying a few nights at a real first-class hotel.

At dinner that night in the hotel dining room, the professor tried to be optimistic about catching up with Father Higgins and freeing him from the thing that had possessed him. But secretly he was near despair. What if Father Higgins had gone on to some other place? And even if he was here in Bristol, it was a city of a third of a million people. Father Higgins could get lost in it like a raindrop in the ocean. Ah well, the professor told himself, we're here. We'll just have to wait and see what happens.

Just as the three of them were having dessert, Johnny leaned over and poked the professor in the arm. *"Look, professor!"* he whispered hoarsely. *"It's him! Over there!"*

The professor turned and looked across the large dining room. Seated at a small round table that was covered with a snowy-white cloth was the horsy-faced, respectable Dr. Masterman. He was quietly sipping an after-dinner brandy and puffing on a cigar.

"God in heaven!" muttered the professor, and tears came to his eyes. He was glad they had found their friend, but it was like finding him ill with some incurable disease. The professor felt helpless, and he hated that feeling more than any in the world.

"Whaddaya think we oughta do?" muttered Fergie.

The professor gritted his teeth and fought to control himself. "There's not much we can do for now," he said quietly. "If we go over there and start bothering that man, we'll get thrown out of the hotel and maybe into jail. And the spirit may have the power to kill Father Higgins. We shouldn't forget about that possibility." The professor fell silent and stared thoughtfully at his plate. Suddenly an idea came to him. "Hmmm . . ." he said, rubbing his chin. "I wonder . . ."

Johnny looked hard at the professor. "What is it?" he asked anxiously.

"Hm?" said the professor absentmindedly. "Oh, it was nothing. At least, it probably is nothing—we'll just have to see. For now, let's finish up and go out for a walk. I don't know if Dr. Masterman has seen us, but maybe he hasn't. There's a side door over there."

Late that night the professor came down to the hotel's library to borrow a book, so he could read himself to sleep. After browsing awhile among the leather-covered volumes, he picked out *Barchester Towers*, which always made him drowsy when he read it. With the book in his hand he stepped out into the dimly lit corridor and headed for the elevator. As usual, the professor walked with his head down, and so he was startled when he ran up against something with a jarring *thump*. Stepping back, he looked up and found that he was staring at Dr. Masterman. The professor turned pale, but he did not back down. Instead he made the sign of the cross in the air and muttered an old Latin prayer that Father Higgins himself had taught him. In English it meant:

> Lord, show us this creature as he really is, not as he seems to be. Banish deceitful visions and let the truth shine forth.

For a second or two nothing happened. Then the air around Dr. Masterman seemed to shimmer, and the professor saw Father Higgins standing there, looking haggard and hollow-eyed. After a blinding flash of light, the professor heard something like a thunderclap inside his head, and he fell to the floor, unconscious.

CHAPTER SIX

The professor awoke in a hospital bed that stood in a sunny corner of a whitewashed room. He was not wearing his glasses, so everything looked out of focus. Two shapes hovered by the bedside, and one reached out to hand him his spectacles. He put them on and saw Johnny and Fergie, who were sitting in chairs and wearing anxious frowns. After an awkward silence Johnny spoke.

"How . . . how are you feeling, professor?" he asked timidly.

The professor winced. "Well, if you must know," he said, "I feel as if someone had picked me up and slammed me against a brick wall. I'll live, though—don't you worry about that! I'll bet you were wondering what on earth happened to me, weren't you?"

Fergie puckered up his mouth. "Well, yeah, prof. The hotel porter found you knocked out on the hall floor, an' he figured you had had a heart attack or somethin' like that. What really happened?"

The professor pulled himself into a sitting position and calmly told them about his encounter with the creature called Dr. Rufus Masterman. "So there we are, gentlemen!" he said. "At least now we know that we were right about Father Higgins's possession. But the big question remains. What does this demon want, and why does he need Father Higgins? I feel like someone waiting for lightning to strike, only I don't know where it will hit."

The professor grew silent. Johnny noticed that a sea gull had landed on the stone ledge outside the window. He watched as it ruffled its feathers and strutted pompously up and down. Finally Fergie spoke up.

"We asked about Dr. Masterman today at the hotel, and the guy said he had checked out. Whaddaya make of that?"

The professor glared. "What do I make of it?" he snapped. "We are stuck for the time being. Bristol has a big railway station, with trains that go to all parts of England. All Masterman has to do is buy a ticket and vanish. He could even hop aboard one of the freighters here in the harbor—sometimes they take passengers. Or he could be living in another part of Bristol and be impossible to find. The only clues we have are those idiotic notes that were sent to Higgy. I tell you what, boys:

I'll go down to the Bristol Public Library and see if I can find anything that connects with these clues. But first we have to move out of the Grand Hotel. It's a nice place, but it's costing a sinful amount of money. We'll find a cheaper place to stay as soon as I can get out of this hospital!"

That evening, about sunset, the boys and the professor arrived at the home of Mr. and Mrs. Lucius O'Trigger on St. Paul's Road. The house was old, three stories high, and made of brown sandstone. Knobby marble ornaments decorated the window sills, and in one window they could see a cardboard bed and breakfast sign. A brick wall with an iron gate surrounded the tiny front yard, which was full of scraggly grass and had a stone fountain with a metal Cupid squatting in the middle. After the professor had paid the taxi driver, they walked up to the front door and rang the bell. The door was opened by a short, bald man in baggy tweed trousers, an unbuttoned vest, and a soiled blue shirt. As soon as he saw his visitors, he smiled and held out his hand.

"Good evening!" he said as he ushered them in. "I'm Mr. O'Trigger, and you must be the three folks from America. Your rooms are on the second floor at the rear. Soap and towels are in the closet at the end of the hall. If you need anything, ask me or the missus. I hope you enjoy your stay here."

The second floor turned out to be the third floor, because English people call the first floor the ground floor and count the next floor as the first. Their three bedrooms were very pleasant and were accessible from a small parlor, which was furnished with comfy, flower-print-covered armchairs and small lamps on tiny round tables. A shelf on the wall held an electric teapot with cups and saucers and a canister of tea. The swing-out windows looked across a deep valley where rows and rows of stone or brick houses stood. Already the mists of evening were gathering outside, and a reddish light tinged the air. After everyone had gotten settled, the professor filled the teapot and plugged it in. Soon they were all sipping strong brown tea around the glass-topped coffee table.

"So what are Johnny and I supposed to do while you're plowin' through stuff at the library, prof?" asked Fergie impatiently.

"If I were you two," said the professor, "I'd wander around and see the sights of this ancient city. There are also some interesting things to see in the towns nearby, and bus fare is cheap."

Fergie and Johnny looked at each other. They both felt frustrated. They wanted to help the professor, but they knew that there was not much they could do. They would just have to wait and hope that he turned up something.

For two days the boys wandered aimlessly around the city of Bristol. They saw the Cabot Tower, the church of St. Mary Redcliffe, and the Clifton suspension bridge. They rode the big green buses that crawled up and down the steep hills of the city. Sometimes they just sat on benches and wondered what the professor was doing. On the third day they took a bus ride over to the city of Bath and looked at the Roman ruins. They caught the 8:10 bus to Bristol as they had planned, and when they got back to the main Green Line Terminal, it was getting dark. Both boys felt tired and also a little depressed, because the professor hadn't yet found anything in the library that would help them. When they got off the bus, the boys found the professor with a taxi waiting for them. The boys could see from the expression on the professor's face that he hadn't yet come up with anything.

As a fine drizzling mist fell, the professor unlocked the door of the O'Trigger house and led the boys up the three flights of stairs to their rooms. Johnny felt incredibly weary, and he thought about how good his bed would feel tonight. After he had washed up in the bathroom, Johnny went to his room and closed the door with a drowsy yawn. Then he walked over to the little window and stood looking at the yellow fog lamps that lit the streets in the valley below. Drizzle still fell, and the pavement was shiny and wet. Although Johnny was dead tired, he could feel nervousness creeping over his body. Why was he tense? He had no idea. Unfastening the window, Johnny stuck his head out and heard the hum of traffic far below. Rain blew in and wet his face, and this seemed to shake him out of his reverie. With a little laugh he shut the window and fastened it again.

Then he took off his glasses and laid them on the bedside table. With a grateful sigh he crawled into bed and pulled the blanket over him. It was a chilly night, and he had turned on the electric fire in the tiny fireplace. Its glass rods glowed orange, and they were the last things that he saw before he drifted off to sleep.

A little after midnight Johnny awoke with a start. He had no idea what had aroused him, but his reaction was sudden and swift. Quickly he jammed his glasses onto his face; then he jumped out of bed and padded across the floor to his suitcase, which stood on a little folding stand near the door. Digging his hand in under the clothes, he pulled out the silver crucifix and chain that Father Higgins had given him years before. Under a tiny crystal bubble in the center of the crucifix were two splinters of wood, pieces of the True Cross that Jesus died on. After slipping the chain over his head, Johnny felt safer but still very edgy and on guard. But what was there to be afraid of in this homey little room in a boardinghouse run by two friendly old people? As he stood wondering, Johnny heard a sound. *Scratch*, *scratch*. It sounded like fingernails clawing at glass. With fear in his heart, Johnny looked toward the dark, rain-spattered window, and he saw a face. A long pale face with dank matted hair and a weepy yellow mustache and beard. It was the face of an old man with burning hungry eyes and sunken cheeks. As Johnny watched in numb terror, the man's hands groped at the panes, and his mouth opened and closed. What was he trying to say? Inside his head Johnny heard a horrible faint whispering, but he could not understand what it said. For what seemed like a long time the nightmarish face hovered outside the window. Then the whispering faded and the sound of scratching grew faint. The face melted slowly into the rainy darkness and was gone.

CHAPTER SEVEN

For a long time Johnny sat on the edge of his bed and shuddered. With closed eyes and arms wrapped around his body, he felt wave after wave of stomach-churning sickness that he could not control. Then, gradually, he calmed down and opened his eyes. He half expected to see something awful sitting by his bedside, but there was nothing. Johnny walked to the door and drew back the bolt. When he peered outside all he saw was the empty hall. Johnny began to wonder if he had had some kind of awful dream. But he had seemed awake, he had felt awake. With a weary shake of his head, he once more pulled off his glasses and got into bed. As he drifted off to sleep, an old rhyme ran through his head:

As I was going up the stair
I met a man who wasn't there.
He wasn't there again today.
I wish, I wish he'd stay away.

Over and over the stupid jingle ran through Johnny's tired brain until sleep overcame him. When he awoke in the morning, bright sunlight danced on the flowered wallpaper and the worn brown rug. Johnny knew that he ought to feel relieved, but he didn't. Fear still gnawed at his insides. With a thoughtful frown he padded down the hall with his toiletries case in his hand.

When he was all washed up and dressed, Johnny went down to the breakfast room on the ground floor. It was a cheerful room with brass plaques and crossed swords on the walls, and little tables covered with checkered cloths. Silently Johnny slid into his seat across from Fergie and the professor, and he tried hard to get interested in the large English breakfast that was served to him: scrambled eggs, sausage, and toast with marmalade. But food didn't interest him much this morning, and he just fiddled with the things on his plate. The professor was always quick to pick up Johnny's moods.

"What's the matter, John?" he asked.

Johnny looked uncertainly from the professor to Fergie. Would his friends laugh at him if he told them about the face at the window? As he was trying to decide what to say, the professor spoke up again.

"You know, John," he said in a strange tone of voice,

) 59 (

"I went out early this morning to buy a newspaper at a store near here, and I got into a conversation with the store owner. He told me the strangest story about things that happened to him and some other people last night. They saw faces—faces of old, fierce-looking men hovering outside second- and third-story windows. They heard hands clawing at windowpanes, and they thought they heard voices—faint, whispery voices saying things they couldn't understand." The professor paused and began to draw lines on the tablecloth with his fork. "Now then," he went on thoughtfully, "if one person has an odd nightmarish experience, it's no great matter. If two have the same experience on the same night, it would really seem bizarre, and people would start talking about telepathy and ESP. But if half a dozen folks think they've seen the same identical thing, you'd have to believe that something pretty darned weird is going on. Did a scary and unexplainable thing happen to you last night?"

Johnny swallowed hard. Hesitantly he told Fergie and the professor about what he had heard and seen.

". . . And I really don't think it was a dream," he said slowly.

The professor nodded solemnly. "I know. None of the other people thought they were dreaming. They all felt that they had seen . . . well, supernatural creatures, ghosts. I can't help wondering if all this has anything to do with Father Higgins and the broken piece of glass and Dr. Masterman."

No one said a word. They could hear bacon sizzling

in the nearby kitchen and the shelf clock ticking quietly. Finally Fergie spoke.

"Well, prof," he said. "You told us to wait till something happened. So now something has happened, but *what can we do about it?*"

"I might have known that you would ask a question like that, Byron," the professor said. "Right at this minute I haven't the vaguest idea of what we can do. If there is a solution to this frightening business, it is probably in the crazy notes, as I've said before, and I just have to keep plugging away at the library till I find something."

Johnny looked troubled. There was something he wanted to ask the professor, but he was afraid of sounding like an idiot. Finally he coughed and said, "Professor?"

"Yes, John? What is it?"

"Well," Johnny began, "if some evil spirit grabbed Father Higgins and wants to use him for evil purposes, why would the spirit leave notes that would help us to stop him?"

The professor smiled. He liked it when Johnny tried to punch holes in his arguments—it was almost like playing chess with him. "I never said that the notes were left by evil spirits," the professor answered. "I think the ghost of the little girl was definitely an evil spirit. Do you know the saying *The devil hath power to assume a pleasing shape?* Well, the little girl was probably the same demonic power that later made Father Higgins take on the shape of Dr. Rufus Masterman. But there are also forces for good in the world. They can't always speak directly, because the powers of evil are fighting them all the way. But some kindly spirit may have left those strange riddling messages in the hope that Father Higgins would decode them and stomp all over the evil power. Unfortunately Father Higgins got stomped himself. But we're still around, and we're not possessed by demons—not yet, anyway. Sooo . . . I think we ought to get ready to *fight*!"

Days dragged past. The professor labored on at the library, and the boys felt more and more useless. They had run out of things to see, so they just sat in the lounge of the boardinghouse and played chess. By now Johnny and Fergie were convinced that the professor would never find out anything, that they would never see Father Higgins again.

One evening something odd happened.

The boys met the professor outside the main door of the Bristol Library at five P.M., as they usually did. All three of them were hungry, so they went to the center of town to find a restaurant. When they were through eating, they decided to walk back to the boardinghouse. The easiest way was to climb the Christmas Steps, a winding stone staircase that led to the heights above the city. Halfway up the steps the professor paused to catch his breath on a stone landing where an old-fashioned streetlamp burned. As he stood panting, the boys looked around, and suddenly they froze. In a narrow, shadowy alley nearby a man was watching them. The light was poor, but the boys could see that the man was bearded, burly, and fairly tall. He wore a double-breasted navy-blue jacket.

For several seconds the boys said nothing—they were too startled to speak. Finally Fergie found his voice.

"Hey prof!" he exclaimed, tugging at the old man's sleeve. "There's somebody watchin' us in that alleyway there!"

The professor whirled around and stared. There was no one there.

"Byron," he said as he glowered at Fergie over the tops of his glasses, "have you been reading too many Hardy Boys adventures?"

"I saw him too, professor," said Johnny timidly. "He really was there! Honest!"

The professor snorted. "Well," he snapped, "it was probably some old bum, and he didn't have anything better to look at than the three of us. Now come on. We'd better keep climbing."

The boys glanced at each other helplessly. When the professor was feeling stubborn, you couldn't make him see anything. They sighed and followed him up the steps.

When they turned on the radio that night, the boys and the professor heard more reports about ghostly apparitions like the one that Johnny had seen days before. People all over the city had seen the hollow-cheeked floating faces, and panic was setting in. The Bristol Police Department was being flooded with phone calls.

Local ghost experts gave the Bristol *Post* their opinions, which the professor felt were worthless. Psychiatrists said that it was a case of people infecting one another with fear. Everybody seemed to have a theory about what was happening, and this enraged the professor.

"Why can't they all keep their traps shut or at least admit that they don't know anything?" he growled as he sat in the parlor one evening. "If all the so-called experts in the world were put on a barge and shoved out to sea, we'd all be better off!"

Fergie and Johnny were sitting nearby eating cream cakes that they had bought at a local bakery.

"Uh . . . prof?" said Fergie cautiously. "Have you figured out anything about those notes?"

The professor glowered at Fergie over the top of his glasses. "If I had," he muttered, "don't you think I would have told you?" And giving his newspaper a shake, he went back to reading. For the time being he was not in a very conversational mood.

The next evening the boys went out after dinner to look at the Clifton suspension bridge, which was a ten-minute walk from the boardinghouse. It was a beautiful old structure, built by the famous engineer Isambard Kingdom Brunel. The bridge leaps across a two-hundred-foot-deep chasm, and far down below the Avon River flows. When the boys got to the park near the bridge, they saw a breathtaking sight: The setting sun shone in between the heavy gray clouds, bathing the stone towers and swooping steel cables of the old bridge in golden light. Johnny and Fergie just stood staring in amazement. As the sun began to sink and the sky darkened, the boys turned to go home. When they got back to the boardinghouse, they saw that a light was on in the parlor on their floor. The professor had gone back to the library after dinner, but the light meant that he had returned.

"I wonder what kind of mood he's in," muttered Johnny as he shoved the creaky iron gate open. "For the last couple of days he hasn't been much fun to live with."

"No, he sure hasn't!" said Fergie with a shake of his head.

When they opened the door of the parlor, they got a shock: The professor sat in an armchair smoking one of his smelly Balkan Sobranie cigarettes. And across from him, in another chair, sat the burly, bearded man who had been watching them from the alley the night before.

"Good evening, boys!" said the professor, waving cheerfully. "I'd like you to meet my brother Humphrey, who is supposed to be dead."

CHAPTER EIGHT

Humphrey Childermass stood up, and the boys got their first good look at him. He was tall and broad, with ruddy cheeks and a grayish beard sprinkled with black hairs. The wrinkles around his eyes showed that he was an old man. In his teeth he clenched the stem of a briar pipe that sent forth curls of fragrant smoke.

"Greetings, lads!" he boomed as he stepped forward to shake their hands. "As my charming brother has pointed out, the reports of my death have been greatly exaggerated."

"He faked his death," said the professor tartly. "Apparently he decided that the world was getting to be too much for him, so he went into hiding. He has come back from the grave because he thinks he can help us.

And in case you're wondering, he has developed his powers of ESP. That's how he knew what we were up to."

Johnny and Fergie stared in amazement. They were too flabbergasted to speak.

Humphrey motioned for the boys to sit down. He puffed at his pipe and looked thoughtfully out the window. Finally he spoke. "I know you boys will have trouble understanding this," he began, "but I have been interested in the case of the De Marisco Knights for a long time."

"The *who?*" said Johnny and Fergie at the same time.

Humphrey laughed. "The De Mariscos were a family of pirates and warriors who once owned the island of Lundy, which is in the mouth of the Bristol Channel, not far from here. They built a castle on the island and terrorized the people for miles around. They were ruthless and cunning men who thought that looting and killing were delightful things to do. Well, a few of them went a bit further than ordinary villainy. Six of them decided to sell their souls to the devil."

Johnny was astonished. "Why . . . why would they do a thing like that?" he asked hesitantly.

"For the usual reasons," the professor put in. "Power. They could become invisible and fly through the air. They could read your mind and possess your body and use it for awful purposes. As you might guess, these knights had to do some pretty nasty things to get these powers, but they wouldn't let anything stand in their way. They wanted to become superhuman beings. But during the Middle Ages, good people got together and decided to put an end to their activities."

Fergie looked mystified. "How did they do that?"

"No one is sure how it was done," answered Humphrey. "But according to the old stories, they were placed under a magic spell and trapped in an underground room with thick stone walls. Unfortunately one of the six knights got away. He died a natural death, but his spirit wandered the earth restlessly, waiting for a chance to set his fellow knights free. As far as I can figure out, the spirit is the thing that calls itself Dr. Rufus Masterman."

Johnny and Fergie gasped. They looked at each other and wondered if Humphrey could possibly be telling the truth.

"In case you're doubtful," the professor added, "Humphrey and I have put our information together, and we think we're right. The legends tell of a magic stained-glass circle that had something to do with the imprisonment of these knights. And they say that the knight who escaped was named Rufus."

Johnny felt a chill, and he thought of the haggard face that he had seen outside his window. "Have . . . have the knights been turned loose in the world again?" he asked in a faltering voice.

Humphrey shook his head firmly. "No. Not quite," he said. "Masterman must have gone to the place where they are buried in order to set their spirits free. That is why people have been seeing strange things lately. However, the spirits of the knights are harmless without their bodies. They can only frighten. Right now I imagine that the evil Dr. Masterman is waiting for a chance to free the bodies of his long-dead friends from their tomb. And if he does that, horrible things will happen. A pack of vicious, merciless, bloodthirsty creatures will be turned loose on the world."

Humphrey frowned grimly, and everyone was silent. After several minutes Fergie spoke up. He sounded skeptical.

"Look, Mr. Childermass," he said, "if this Rufus Whatsisname can turn loose the spirits of his buddies, why can't he turn loose their bodies?"

Humphrey shrugged. "I'm not sure why. Maybe Father Higgins is resisting him. Even though he's possessed, maybe he still has a mind of his own, sort of, and that mind may be fighting against doing something evil. Or maybe Masterman has to wait until a certain time to do his dirty work—magic has its rules, and they have to be followed. The important thing is that we still may have some time to stop something ghastly from happening. And here's what we have to do: We have to go to the isle of Lundy, find the room where these knights are trapped, and fix things so that they will never ever bother the world again."

Johnny's eyes shone, and he began to get excited. Years ago he had read about Lundy in *National Geographic*. The island was about three miles long, and it had all sorts of odd rock formations as well as the ruins of an old castle. In the 1930's a man named Harman had owned Lundy, and he had tried to make it a separate country with its own coins and stamps. In the midst of his thoughts, Johnny paused—something was puzzling him.

"Wait a minute!" he exclaimed. "How come you think that's where the tomb of the knights is?"

The professor smiled smugly. "Well, we're not absolutely sure," he said, "but that's where the knights came from. And Lundy is the solution to one of those notes. Remember *bustard custard* and *drake cake*? Well, how about puffin muffins?"

"Puffin *what*?" asked Fergie. "What are you talkin' about?"

Johnny knew. Suddenly he remembered that puffins nested all over the isle of Lundy. Puffins are large birds with bodies like ducks, big feathery ruffs around their faces, and enormous curved beaks. Harman had put puffins on the Lundy stamps and coins that he had issued. Patiently Johnny explained all this to Fergie, who looked at him as if he didn't believe one word he was saying.

"Young John is correct," put in Humphrey with a kind smile. "In fact, in the old Norse language *Lund Y* means Puffin Island. There's always the possibility, I suppose, that we're going on a wild goose chase, but I don't think so, and neither does Roderick. I'm not exactly sure what we'll do when we find the tomb of the knights, but the riddles on those other scraps of paper may help us to figure that out. Are you boys ready for a short ocean voyage out to the mouth of the stormy Bristol Channel?"

Fergie and Johnny looked at each other. They imagined themselves in a rowboat, being pitched about by mountainous waves. But they were not about to admit that they were scared, so they nodded and said that they wanted to go.

"Fine!" said Humphrey, rubbing his hands enthusiastically. "And now I'd like to invite you all over to my house for dinner."

As it turned out, Humphrey lived just on the other side of the Clifton suspension bridge. His house was made of yellowish stone with steep Gothic gables and fancy carved wooden decorations on the eaves. Tall brick chimneys rose above the trees that crowded about the house, and on the front porch were stacks of broken chairs. Inside, the house smelled of wood smoke and damp paper, and in the enormous living room logs crackled in the fireplace. A large threadbare Oriental rug covered the floor, and leather-covered chairs and couches stood grouped together. Steins and old tarnished silver trophies littered the mantelpiece and the built-in shelves of the walls, and piles of books could be seen in the shadowy corners of the room. Some of these books were very large and had ribbed vellum covers. Johnny wanted to know what was in them, but he was too shy to ask.

Dinner was served at the kitchen table, and it was

delicious. Cold roast beef and tongue, Stilton and Cheshire cheeses, homemade bread, fresh lettuce, and cherry tomatoes. For the boys there were Cokes, and for the two men Newcastle brown ale. On the table was a tiny pot of Coleman's mustard, and the boys soon found that a little of it went a long way. For dessert Humphrey served a sherry trifle that he had made himself: lots of little cubes of cake soaked in sherry and covered with fruit and whipped cream. After the meal Humphrey and the professor took their coffee into the living room, where they sat for hours, talking about old times. The boys went to the recreation room, which had two pinball machines, a pool table, and an oblong overhead light with green fringe around its shade. Fergie was a hotshot pool player, and Johnny knew he couldn't compete with him. But they played anyway and enjoyed themselves very much.

Finally it was time to go. The professor and the boys bade Humphrey good-bye, and they walked down the path between the trees to the sidewalk that led to the bridge. Fog had drifted into the city, and eerie haloes hung around the streetlamps. As the three of them started across the bridge, a stiff wind began to blow. The old bridge groaned and creaked in the wind. By the time they got to the middle of the bridge, the wind had turned into a roaring gale, and the boys and the professor had to cling to the iron handrail as they inched forward.

"My . . . this is . . . incredible," gasped the professor

as he struggled along. "I don't think . . . we're going to make it to . . . the . . ."

His voice was lost in the shrieking of the wind. Far ahead, on the other side of the bridge, a tall, gaunt figure could be seen standing under a streetlamp. It looked like a man in an overcoat and narrow-brimmed hat. Mists swirled about the figure, who now raised his hand and made a strange sign in the air. The wind began to blow harder. Johnny was slammed against the railing, which was only about chest high. He found that incredibly, he was being lifted up by unseen forces. A few minutes more and he would be hurled headlong two hundred feet to his death.

CHAPTER NINE

Slowly Johnny felt his body moving up the railing. He clung desperately to the iron bar, closed his eyes tight, and prayed. In his ears the wild wind boomed, and he was so frightened that he was afraid he would black out. How long could he hang on? Would he lose consciousness before he hit the stones that lay far below? But suddenly a loud voice rose above the howling storm:

> I wish the wind may cease to roar,
> No thrashing of the flood.
> By him that harrowed hell I swear
> And by the holy rood!

The wind died, and Johnny slid gasping to the riveted iron walkway of the bridge. Stunned, he looked around and saw the professor and Fergie not far from him. They were kneeling with their hands over their faces, and both of them seemed to be sobbing. Walking toward them from the far end of the bridge was Humphrey. He strode briskly along, and as he went he hummed a jaunty little tune. When Humphrey got to the place where his brother was kneeling, he bent and helped him up. With a lot of sneezing and harrumphing, the professor pulled himself together. He didn't like to have people see him in a weepy state, so he tried to hide his feelings as well as he could. He was glad to be alive.

"Goodness!" he exclaimed, mopping his face with his handkerchief. "I have never felt anything like that in my life! Another few seconds and—" He paused and glared accusingly at his brother. "Humphrey!" he roared. "You know magic spells! And you never told me!"

Humphrey smiled modestly and bowed. "I never like to brag about my accomplishments," he said. "But I'm glad I was able to save you. A few seconds after you left the house, I sensed his presence, and I'm glad I came as fast as I did."

"Presence?" growled the professor. "Presence? Whose presence?"

Humphrey sighed and looked down toward the other end of the bridge, where a streetlamp burned quietly in the fog. "Masterman's," he said with a sour grimace. "I should have known that he would be capable of doing something like this. As long as he lives inside Father

Higgins's body, he is a menace. Some of his ancient powers must have returned to him, and who knows what he is capable of now? Luckily, I have a few little tricks of my own."

"I'll say!" said Fergie, gazing admiringly at Humphrey. "I thought we were all goners!"

"You very nearly were," said Humphrey gravely. "But see here! I think you had better come back and spend the night at my place. It's not absolutely one-hundred-percent safe, but it's a lot safer than your place. Masterman knows you're onto him, and he's afraid you'll mess up his plans. He'll be back—you can be sure of that. But for the time being our little duel may have scared him off. Come on. Let's go."

No one needed to be persuaded. With grateful smiles the boys and the professor tramped back across the bridge to Humphrey's house, where Humphrey showed them all to their rooms. The huge oak beds were inviting, and in each room a portable electric heater was plugged into the wall. Johnny's heater had a plastic front made to look like heaps of coal, and behind the coals a red light flickered. In spite of the musty sheets, the room seemed warm and cozy, and Johnny fell asleep thinking about how Humphrey had stood on the bridge uttering words of power to drive the forces of darkness away.

The next day was a very busy one. The professor paid their bill at the O'Triggers' house, and Humphrey found out about a small ferry that sailed between a town called

Ilfracombe and the isle of Lundy. Then Humphrey packed a tent, a Coleman lamp, sleeping bags, and a portable stove, which he had used camping in Wales. He pointed out that these things might be necessary— Lundy had only forty people living on it, and there was only one small inn. Finally all the arrangements were made, and in the afternoon, Humphrey rolled his old, mud-spattered Bentley out of the garage. It was a windy day, with tattered clouds flying across the sky. A storm had been predicted, but Humphrey remained optimistic, and he whistled cheerfully as he helped the others load their equipment into the car. Johnny and Fergie climbed into the roomy backseat, and the two men got into the front. Soon they were on narrow back roads that ran between high stone walls or rows of hedges. Humphrey was just as terrifying a driver as the professor was, and the boys were hurled all over the backseat as the car careened around curves. The sky began to get darker and thunder rumbled in the distance. Trees and bushes thrashed in a wind that suddenly sprang up, and rain fell in big drops that splatted on the windshield. Soon the rain was falling in sheets, and the car slowed to a crawl. Humphrey turned on his headlights and began to bravely sing "The Three Fishers," an old song about some fishermen who got drowned in a storm at sea:

> . . . And the night rack came rolling in
> ragged and brown.

For men must work, and women must weep
Though storms be sudden and waters be deep
And the harbor bar be moaning. . . .

"You have great taste in songs," said the professor sarcastically. "How long do you think this blasted storm is going to last?"

Humphrey shrugged. "Search me. Sometimes they go on for days in these parts. It's sea weather, because we're so close to the coast. If it's storming this hard when we reach Ilfracombe, the ferry may not be able to take us to Lundy today."

"Peachy," grumbled the professor. "So what do we do in that case?"

"We wait—that's all we can do. But there is one good thing—if we can't get to Lundy, then neither can Masterman—unless of course he's out there already."

Johnny shivered and looked out at the pouring rain. "Do you think he's waiting for us somewhere, professor?" he asked in a quavering voice.

"Anything's possible," put in Humphrey. "Especially when you're dealing with the ghost of a sorcerer. But I hope I'll be equal to the old buzzard, whatever he tries to pull. As I said, I have some knowledge of magic arts, though I certainly am not a wizard."

The car crawled up and down hills, as the rain fell steadily and the car's yellow fog lamps sent their beams out into the dark. After another hour the Bentley came rolling into the pleasant little fishing port of Ilfracombe—except that it didn't look all that pleasant, with a driving rain falling and wind whipping the harbor water into a fury of white froth. Carefully Humphrey nosed the car into a narrow, winding street and pulled up in front of a respectable-looking red-brick hotel. Two gas lamps burned outside the door, and a wooden sign creaked and swung in the wind. On the sign was a picture of a stuffy-looking British navy officer in a cocked hat, blue uniform, and gold epaulets, and the name of the hotel—the Admiral Hood Inn.

Humphrey turned off the engine and sat staring at the raindrops that danced on the hood of the car. "Well, here we are," he said wearily. "This is a very nice hotel—I've stayed here before. We can't get to Lundy tonight. God only knows when this awful weather will let up."

The professor patted his brother on the arm. "What can't be helped can't be helped," he said gently. "You've done all you could, Humphrey, and more besides. Let's hope tomorrow we'll wake up to clear skies and a quiet sea. In the meantime, let's go in and find some rooms. I don't know about the rest of you, but I'm good for dinner and not much more."

The boys followed the two men into the inn. As it turned out, there were two adjoining rooms available— one for the boys and one for the professor and his brother. After the four of them had gotten checked in, Humphrey led the way down the street to a restaurant. By eight in the evening everyone was sitting around in the hotel's lounge, watching television or leafing through magazines. And by ten they were all sound asleep.

Johnny and Fergie shared a low-ceilinged room with framed engravings of hunting dogs on the walls. The windows were half open, so they fell asleep to the sound of rain pattering in the courtyard behind the inn. Afterward Johnny never could figure out what it was that awoke him. But around 3 A.M. he came awake with a start and sat upright in his bed, glancing around and wondering what was the matter. A few feet away Fergie snored on. Carefully, Johnny put his glasses on. He could not shake off the feeling that there was something very wrong. With a worried frown on his face, he got up and padded across the rug to the door that led to the room where Humphrey and the professor were sleeping. As quietly as he could, Johnny twisted the knob and peered inside. The room wasn't completely dark, with light from a streetlamp filtering in. Johnny could see two empty beds covered with rumpled sheets. And the door leading to the hall was ajar. The men had gone! But where to, and why?

Johnny felt cold all over, but he managed to pull himself together. Stiffly he marched back into the other room and started shaking Fergie.

"Wha . . . what the . . ." mumbled Fergie thickly. He brushed his hair out of his eyes and then sat up. "What's goin' on?" he grumbled irritably. "Is the hotel on fire?"

"They're gone!" whispered Johnny. "Humphrey and the professor are gone! They're not in their room!"

Fergie yawned. "Maybe they couldn't sleep, so they went out to catch a late movie."

Johnny shook his head. "No, no, that's not possible!" he said. "Everything in these English towns shuts down early—you know that as well as I do. And the weather outside is terrible. They didn't go for a walk. Fergie, I'm scared—I mean it!"

Wearily, Fergie peeled back the sheet and swung his legs out of the bed. He sat there with his hands on his knees, staring glumly up at Johnny. "Well, what are we supposed to do?" he asked. "Run around the streets hollering for them? They might've just wanted to have a private talk somewhere. I think you're pushin' the panic button a little early, big John!"

Johnny folded his arms and frowned stubbornly. "Look, Fergie," he said, "if you don't want to come with me to look for them, I'll go by myself!"

Fergie sighed. Johnny usually was pretty timid, but when he got stubborn, he was impossible to move. "Oh, all right!" Fergie growled. "I'll come with you. Just let me get some clothes on, okay?"

A few minutes later Fergie and Johnny were standing in the doorway of the old inn, staring out at the falling rain. Both were wearing raincoats, and Johnny was carrying the professor's large black umbrella.

"He didn't take this with him, either," muttered

Johnny, tapping the fabric of the umbrella with his finger. "That's not like the professor—you know he hates to get his head wet!"

Fergie shrugged. "Okay, okay, you made your point! Something funny is going on. So which way do we go to look for 'em?"

Johnny paused. With a strange look on his face, he unbuttoned the front of his raincoat and reached in under his shirt to touch the silver crucifix that hung from a chain around his neck. Then he pulled out his hand, buttoned the raincoat again, and pointed off to the right. "This way," he said.

Fergie gave Johnny one of his you-must-be-out-of-your-mind looks. But he followed his friend down the street. Johnny put up the umbrella, and the rain made a steady noise on the stiff cloth. They walked past dark, closed-up shops. In the distance the boys saw a lighted storefront.

"Hey, whaddaya make of that?" whispered Fergie, pointing. "Somebody must be cleanin' their store or something like that."

Johnny said nothing and plodded onward. They crossed a small intersection and felt rough cobblestones under their feet. Soon they were close to the lighted store and could see shelves full of bottles behind the plate-glass window. All kinds of bottles—short ones, fat ones, tall skinny ones, whiskey bottles, medicine bottles, and tiny ointment bottles. They came in all colors, mauve and blood red, dark blue and green and purple. All were covered with cobwebs. The light inside the store cast varied patterns of color on the sidewalk outside. As he paused in front of the shop, Johnny looked up, and his blood froze. The weathered wooden sign over the door said MASTERMAN'S BOTTLE SHOP.

After swallowing hard a couple of times, Johnny forced himself to move closer. Fergie was right beside him. They saw a hand-printed cardboard sign taped to the oblong window of the door. It said SPECIAL TODAY. PESTS IN SMALL CONTAINERS.

For a long time the two boys paused outside the dusty door. Then, with a sudden motion, Johnny moved boldly forward and twisted the knob, and they stepped inside. The place looked deserted. Shadowy bundles lay scattered on the bare boards of the floor, and in the air was a sickening smell of mold. Light came from two bare bulbs that hung from the ceiling by knotted black cords, and at the back of the shop was a counter made of rough, unvarnished planks. Two bottles stood on the counter, and there seemed to be something inside them. Suddenly a figure stepped forward from the deep shadows behind the counter. It was Dr. Masterman, and his long, horsy face was lit by a pale, trembling light. He grinned evilly and motioned for the boys to come toward him. They obeyed—they had to. It was as if there were collars around their necks and someone was tugging at them. Fergie and Johnny stood before the counter, and they

) 83 (

saw what was in the bottles. The wide, distorted face of the professor looked out from one; from the other Humphrey stared. On each face was a look of despair and fear.

CHAPTER TEN

Rooted to the spot, frozen in place by fear, Johnny and Fergie stared at the two bottles. The face of Dr. Masterman floated in the darkness like something seen in a dream. Then thunder burst inside the heads of the boys, and they fell unconscious to the floor.

How long they lay there neither of them knew. But when they awoke, they found the shop dark and deserted. The front door was open and banged gently in the damp, salty-smelling breeze. Moonlight streamed in through the dusty windows, and it was clear that the storm was over. As their eyes got used to the darkness, the boys saw that a thick layer of dust lay over the warped boards of the floor. The counter was bare, and the shelves where bottles had stood were bare also. The shadowy shapes they had seen earlier turned out to be piles of junk. With a great effort Johnny pulled himself to his feet. He felt light-headed and nauseated, like someone who has just gotten out of bed after a long illness. Stooping, he tugged gently at Fergie's arm, and at last his friend got up too. Fergie looked pale and groggy, and beads of sweat stood out on his forehead. But he soon pulled himself together and clenched his fists. He looked angry.

"That rotten thing!" he said. "I'm gonna make him pay if it's the last thing I do!" But then he realized that his words were foolish, and tears came to his eyes. "What are we gonna do now?" he asked in a quavering voice. "Why didn't he just kill us and get it over with? He tried to kill us back at the bridge, didn't he? So why did he let us go this time?"

Johnny thought a bit. "I think that even evil spirits can change their minds," he said slowly. "He must've decided that we weren't worth bothering with. Besides, it probably gave him a big thrill to have us see what had happened to our friends. Especially since he knows darned well that we can't do a thing about it."

Fergie looked bewildered. "Do you really think the prof and Humphrey are still alive?"

Johnny frowned stubbornly. "Yes. I really do. They're off in some other dimension, and God knows what Masterman is doing to them. For a sadistic creep like that, it'd be more fun to torture people than to kill them.

But the game isn't over yet! We've got to try to rescue them!"

Fergie laughed scornfully. "Rescue them! That's a good one! We'll be lucky if we get back home in one piece! How're we gonna rescue them?"

Johnny bit his lip. "I don't know yet how we're gonna do that," he said after a short pause. "But the professor always says that you can solve a lot of mysteries just by using what you know. We have those weird notes that were sent to Father Higgins, and we have all that stuff that Humphrey told us. So I think we should pack up and go out to the isle of Lundy as soon as we can."

Fergie was totally flabbergasted. He always thought of Johnny as a scaredy-cat, and he kidded him about this often. But here was his friend suggesting that the two of them go out and finish the work that the men had started. It seemed absolutely crazy.

For a while Fergie couldn't think of anything to say. He sighed and shook his head. Then he walked over to the counter and began drawing circles in the dust with his finger. "I wanta get those two old guys back just as much as you do," he said slowly. "Humphrey and the prof know a lot more than we do, and maybe they could have figured out some way to settle Masterman's hash once we got out to that dumb island. But we're just a couple of kids. If Masterman figures out that we're after him, we're liable to wind up in a couple of bottles ourselves. And then what'll we do?"

Johnny's face had frozen into a mask of grim determination. "Okay, Fergie, thanks a lot," he said, through his teeth. "I'll go out there by myself."

That did it. Fergie looked at Johnny for a few seconds, and then he turned and pounded his fists on the counter. "Oh, all *right!*" he exclaimed in desperation. "I'll go out there with you, but if you get me killed, I'm gonna hate you!"

Johnny grinned, and tears came to his eyes. He knew that his stouthearted friend would not let him down. "Come on!" he whispered, motioning toward the door. "We'd better get back to the hotel. Do you know what time it is?"

Fergie peered at the luminous dial of his watch. "It's a little after four in the morning," he said. "Do you know when the ferryboat leaves?"

Johnny shook his head. "No. But the professor had a timetable—it's probably in his room somewhere. Let's just hope that the weather stays good for us!"

When the boys got back to the hotel, they went straight up to their room and started packing. Fergie stuffed things into the backpack that he used for a suitcase, and Johnny found the ferryboat schedule on the professor's bed. It said that a small steamboat named *The Duke of Clarence* would leave at 6:10 A.M. from Fanshawe's Pier, whatever that was. Finally, when their own things were packed, the boys rooted through the professor's suitcase to see if they could find anything useful. Luckily, the professor carried cash and not traveler's checks, and the boys found a big wad of five- and ten-pound notes tucked in under some of his shirts. Johnny found a book called *History of England* lying open on the bedside table. The chapter heading in heavy black print, "The Funeral of King Charles the First," caught his eye. For a moment Johnny was puzzled, but then he remembered one of the mysterious notes that had been sent to Father Higgins: *Remember the funeral of King Charles the First.* So he threw the book into his suitcase, along with the typewritten sheet that contained the whole list of mysterious messages.

"Well, I guess that's about it, John baby," said Fergie as he glanced around the room. "We've got our passports and some money, an' maybe we better go out to the car and get a couple of flashlights and some rope. The prof said this was a rocky island with a lot of steep cliffs, so maybe we will have to do some climbing."

Johnny felt his stomach turn over. He was scared of heights, and he had never done any kind of rock climbing in his life. But if he had to climb, then he would. After a quick look around the room the boys left, closing the door softly behind them. Quietly they padded down the carpeted staircase of the inn and out the front door. The air outside felt chilly and fresh, and the sun was just beginning to rise. Fergie had a good sense of direction, and he remembered the route they had taken when they entered the town.

"I think the docks must be off that way," he said,

pointing to the left. "But first we have to go to the car. It'll just take a minute."

Fergie dug Humphrey's keys out of his pocket—he had found them on a bedside table. He opened the trunk and pulled out the professor's black leather satchel. From it he took a coil of rope, two nickel-plated flashlights, and a tire iron that he might be able to use as a crowbar. After stuffing these things into his backpack, Fergie locked the trunk and marched briskly down the sidewalk, with Johnny beside him. They crossed the street and found a dirt path bordered by whitewashed stones, which led to a dock with a little wooden shed next to it. The sign on the shed's roof said FANSHAWE'S PIER. A small ticket window at one end of the shed was open, and behind it sat a bored-looking old man in a blue shirt.

"What'll it be, lads?" he asked in a thick Scottish accent. "Off to the islands, eh?"

Johnny pulled out his wallet and asked for two round-trip tickets to Lundy. They were a pound apiece, so he peeled off two green pound notes and gave them to the man. In return the boys got four pink tickets, and they were told to wait on the dock. The steamer would be along very soon.

Fergie and Johnny walked farther along the path and out onto the weathered boards of the dock. They saw that three other people were waiting for the ferry to Lundy. There were two women in cloth coats and scarves, and a man in a tweed suit. The boys were very relieved to see that Dr. Masterman was not there, though they had a pretty good idea that he would show up eventually to perform some black magic on Lundy to set those evil ghostly knights free. The boys paced impatiently back and forth. Fergie glanced at his watch every few minutes, and he began wondering if the boat would ever come. Finally, at a little after six, the boys heard the loud hooting of a steam whistle, and a small white steamship with a single black smokestack came chugging into the harbor. It pulled up next to the dock, and sailors fastened it in place with ropes wound around posts. Then a gangplank came clattering down, and the passengers filed on board.

The trip took a little over an hour. Johnny spent most of the time sitting on a bench and reading *History of England,* which he had brought along. Fergie just sat humming tunelessly and staring off into space.

"You know what, Fergie?" said Johnny suddenly. "King Charles's funeral was kind of interesting. He got his head cut off, and his friends put him in a coffin and took him to an ancient church to bury him. They wanted to put him in the burial vault under the church's floor, only they didn't know where it was. So they stomped on the floor until they heard a hollow sound. Then they pried up the stone, and sure enough, there was this underground room. Do you think we're gonna have to do something like that to find out where those knights are buried?"

Fergie pursed his lips. "I guess so. But I wish one of those handy-dandy clues would tell us what we're supposed to do to stop Masterman. I mean, suppose we get into this hidden room—then what? I don't know any magic spells, and neither do you. What can we really do?"

Johnny wished that he had an answer, but he didn't. He just sat silently poring over the book until the steam whistle blew, and he looked up to see the isle of Lundy rising before him. From reading *National Geographic* Johnny knew it was oblong, and they could see it was covered with tall crags and shelves of rock. Above the crags seemed to be a grassy plain, and at one end of the island the ruins of a castle could be seen. The boat glided into Lundy's only harbor. Here, nestled under the dark, looming rocks, were a few houses and a small stone church. The island looked desolate and forbidding, even in bright sunshine, and the boys felt a tightening in their stomachs as the steamer came alongside the stone pier. Silently they trudged down the gangplank, and after asking for directions, they made their way to the island's only inn. It was a plain two-story stone house, and when Fergie and Johnny walked in the front door, the innkeeper seemed very surprised to see them. He was a ruddy-faced man with wildly sprouting side whiskers, and he wore a turtleneck sweater and worn corduroy trousers.

"Greetings, lads!" he said with a grin. "Are you visiting relatives?"

Quickly Johnny made up a story. "I . . . we came out

to see the island," he began. "Our folks didn't want to come, so we just took the trip ourselves."

The innkeeper's grin got wider. "You Yanks are pretty independent, aren't you? Well, welcome to Lundy, isle of puffins and former lair of the piratical De Marisco family. You wouldn't by chance be wanting a room for the night, would you?"

Johnny and Fergie were delighted. They had thought that they would have to camp out in the open, and if it rained, they'd get soaked. Quickly Johnny pulled out his wallet and handed over the money for a double room. After they put their bags behind the counter, the innkeeper led the boys to the breakfast room, where they sat down and ate.

"Well, John baby, we made it this far," said Fergie with a confident smile. "Now if we can just stay out of the way of Filthy J. Nasty, all will be well."

"Yeah," said Johnny, glancing nervously around the room. "There's another boat that's supposed to arrive at noon. I'll bet you he'll be on it."

"You're probably right," said Fergie as he buttered a muffin. "I wouldn't give two cents for our chances if we run into him, and you know he'll probably stay at this hotel. Maybe we better stick our bags in the room and go poke around on the island. I wanta see if we can find that underground room."

Johnny glanced nervously toward the door. "What if he's waiting for us when we come back? What'll we do?"

Fergie shrugged and tried to look brave. "We'll think of something," he said. Then he added sarcastically, "Anyways, you have that wonderful magic amulet that you wear around your neck. Don't forget about that."

Johnny frowned. He knew that Fergie didn't believe in the powers of the silver crucifix, and this bothered him. It was reassuring, however, to be reminded of its existence, and he patted his shirt front to make sure it was still there.

After breakfast the boys went out to explore Lundy. They struggled up a steep rocky path that led to the grassy plain on top of the island. After resting a bit, they wandered around for a while, peering down at the dark shelves of rock. Johnny remembered a lot from the *National Geographic* article about Lundy, and he searched for some of the curious rock formations that are scattered about the island. At the edge of a cliff he discovered the Logan Stone, which is shaped like a child's top. At one time it had balanced perfectly on its pointed tip, but a tourist had rocked it with a crowbar, and now it lay propped against the granite wall of the cliff. After they had inspected the stone, Fergie wanted to look at the ruins of the castle. Soon they were walking inside the tall, ragged walls of the fortress that had once protected the De Marisco pirates. In one corner of the ruins they found the entrance to a roofless chapel. Johnny gasped.

"Oh my gosh!" he cried, pointing. "Look, Fergie!"

At first Fergie did not understand what Johnny was

so worked up about. But then he moved closer, and he could see it too. Stone heads were carved on the arched doorway. They had once been meant to look like saints and kings and queens, but centuries of wind and rain had worn the carved faces till they were featureless.

"This is the church of the faceless images!" Johnny whispered in an awestruck tone. "It has to be! Come on, let's go inside."

They marched through the doorless arch. Crumbling walls rose on both sides, and empty pointed windows stared down at them. Grass grew in cracks between the stones of the floor. At the far end of the little church a mossy altar table still stood. Johnny began to feel very creepy and nervous. If their guesses were right, they were walking on top of the underground room where the evil knights were buried. Johnny imagined ghostly forms in tattered garments rising up through the floor of the chapel, and he shivered.

Fergie glanced at Johnny quickly. "What's the matter?" he asked. "You thinkin' about those knights Humphrey told us about?"

Johnny nodded.

"Well, don't worry for now," Fergie muttered. "They can't do anything in the daylight. Anyway, that's the way it always works in vampire movies."

Johnny looked doubtful. Knights didn't have to follow the rules of movie vampires. Uneasily, he peered around at the broken arches and empty, staring windows. This was the place—it had to be. And Masterman would be coming soon to set his fellow creatures free. It was up to good old Johnny Dixon and his pal Fergie to stop the evil sorcerer.

Johnny felt very depressed. How could they possibly do anything to hurt Masterman? But then he set his jaw and tried to feel powerful. Humphrey, the professor, and Father Higgins had all been imprisoned by Masterman's evil magic. Somehow he and Fergie would have to find a way to set them free.

CHAPTER ELEVEN

Fergie and Johnny began studying the floor. The stone slabs were square and had been fitted together without mortar or cement. Fergie knelt down and found that moss grew in only some of the spaces between the stones. Other stones were fitted so tightly together that he was unable to slip the blade of his knife into the cracks.

"I wish I had brought that tire iron with me," Fergie muttered as he pulled himself to his feet. "We could use it to pound on the stones to find out where that room is."

"If there is a room," Johnny added quietly. The longer he hung around this place, the more doubtful he became. He had been scared at first, but his fear had melted away, and now all sorts of questions came crowding into his mind: Humphrey's tale of the underground room was just a legend, and legends weren't always true. What if Masterman wasn't coming out to Lundy at all? What if he had just snatched away their friends to show how powerful he was? Maybe there weren't any knights— maybe those ghostly faces had been conjured up by the evil Masterman. If that were true, then he and Fergie were out here on a wild goose chase, and Masterman was free to do anything. . . . But what happened when he got tired of using Father Higgins's body and decided to kill the priest? When he decided to send the professor and Humphrey into the black void, where they would be forever? A cold wind began to blow into the chapel through the empty arches, and Johnny trembled.

Fergie stomped on some of the stones, but none sounded hollow. Dejectedly, the two boys made their way out of the chapel and down the rocky path that led to the little village. They both were hungry, and they ate lunch at the inn. Afterward they returned to the chapel, but the professor's tire iron didn't produce any hollow sounds either. Feeling tired and glum, they sat cross-legged on the grass and watched the sea and the birds, and soon fell asleep with the yelping of sea gulls ringing in their ears. When they woke up, it was four in the afternoon, so the two of them went back to their hotel room and played chess for a while. The strain of waiting for Masterman was beginning to get to them. Every time they heard the hooting of a steam whistle, they rushed to the window to see who was getting off the ferry. Dinnertime came, and the boys ordered roast beef and Yorkshire pudding. Then they decided to take a stroll around the island, which by now was becoming very familiar to them.

"If I lived here all the time, I think I would go out of my ever-loving mind," said Fergie as they clambered down the rocky path once again. "They don't even have television sets! What do you think they do in the winter? Catch up on their sleep?"

"Oh, dry up, Fergie!" grumbled Johnny. "I'm just as tired of this place as you are. Tomorrow we'll go back to that fishing-port town and see if we can figure out how to get home. We have about two thousand dollars of the professor's money, and our airplane tickets and passports, that ought to get us back."

Johnny hung his head. He felt weary and discouraged, and he wished very much that he was back in his grandparents' house in Duston Heights and that he had never heard of magic pieces of stained glass, entombed knights, or the isle of Lundy. He thought of the professor . . . Father Higgins . . . Humphrey . . . and his thoughts turned to despair. Someday he hoped he'd recover from this awful trip, but it would take a long time. A very long time.

The boys spent part of the evening walking on top of the crags. Then a storm came sweeping in, amid rumblings of thunder and lightning flashes. Fergie and Johnny hid under a rock ledge while the rain poured down, and when the storm was over, they made their way back to the inn. After a late snack and some more chess, they went to bed. But around midnight Johnny was awakened by the sound of the steamboat's whistle. Groggily he jammed his glasses on and stumbled to the tiny window. The night sky was crowded with stars, and Johnny could hear the soft hushing sound of the waves. A ferryboat was tied up at the pier, and ghostly puffs of steam rose from its smokestack. A single shadowy figure stood on the dock. It looked like a tall man in a narrow-brimmed hat, with a briefcase in his hand. The man glanced around and then headed toward the path that led to the grassy plain above the town. His shape melted into the shadows and disappeared.

Johnny shuddered and stepped back from the window. Panic was rising inside him—what on earth should he do? After a brief hesitation he ran to Fergie's bed and began to shake him violently.

"Fergie! Fergie! Wake up!" Johnny gasped. "He's here! Masterman is here!"

Woozily Fergie shook himself awake. He pulled his body into a sitting position and rubbed his hands over his face. "Wha . . . what is goin' on anyway?" he muttered thickly. "Where's the fire?"

Johnny knelt by Fergie's bed and whispered excitedly into his ear. "Masterman is here! Wake up! For gosh sakes wake up!"

Suddenly Fergie sat bolt upright. He shook his head

to clear it. "He is? Well, we better get busy. Let's follow the creep an' see what he's up to!"

Gently Johnny laid his hand on Fergie's shoulder. "Just a minute," he said. "Before we take off after him, we oughta protect ourselves."

Fergie was mystified. "Protect? What the devil are you talking about?"

"I mean the silver crucifix," cried Johnny. "The one with the pieces of the True Cross in it. If we both hang on to the crucifix, maybe Masterman won't know we're sneaking up on him. It's worth a try. What do you think?"

Fergie decided that he did not want to tell Johnny what he thought. But he dragged himself out of bed and started putting his clothes on. In a few minutes the two of them were ready to go. Fergie slung his backpack on his shoulder, each one grabbed a flashlight, and they padded down the front staircase and out the front door. The boys passed a short row of dark houses, and then they began to climb the rocky path. They didn't dare turn on their flashlights yet, but the starlight showed the way. Up, up they went, past shelves of rock that seemed about to topple on them. Finally they reached the grassy plain. The gaunt ruins of the De Marisco castle rose, outlined against the night sky. As the boys walked softly along, they appeared to be holding hands— each one had a thumb and finger pressed to part of the silver crucifix. Johnny felt his stomach tighten into a knot of fear.

"I wish I knew where Masterman is," he whispered, as he peered nervously from side to side. "What if he jumps us?"

Fergie chuckled hoarsely. "You shoulda thought about that before, John baby," he whispered. "Just wave this silver gizmo at him an' he'll go away. There's nothing to worry about—we'll just end up in the X-dimension for the next thousand years."

Johnny said nothing. The grass whipped around their pant legs as they walked. They entered the castle as quietly as they could. Still clinging to the crucifix, they sidled along one wall and crept, ever so slowly, toward the entrance of the chapel. When he got to the archway, Johnny took a deep breath and peered in. At the far end of the chapel a yellowish light flickered. An old-fashioned glass lantern with a lit candle stood on the altar. By its glow the boys could see Dr. Masterman standing behind the altar with his hands folded in front of his face. He seemed to be saying a prayer. Then, with an unearthly grin, he raised his arms above his head and began to sink, straight down. His head disappeared behind the altar and was gone.

For several seconds Johnny and Fergie were silent. Then slowly they began to creep forward. Johnny could feel cold beads of sweat on his forehead, and he heard his friend breathing hard beside him. They walked around the right side of the altar and then paused. Fergie let go of the crucifix. With his left hand he reached behind him and pulled the tire iron from his backpack.

Then he flicked on the flashlight in his right hand. The large square stones behind the altar looked absolutely untouched.

"I sure get the stupid prize!" grumbled Fergie. "I never tested these stones. Let's see. . . ." Cautiously he reached forward and thumped the tire iron on the granite slabs. A hollow sound arose.

"Hah!" yelled Fergie, and in an instant he was on his knees, prying at the slab with the chisel-shaped end of the tire iron. It was hard work, and Fergie grunted as he put his weight on the iron bar. Dust rose, and finally the slab began to move. Johnny was beside Fergie, pulling at the stone with his hands. The slab rose higher. It was about an inch thick, and when Johnny got his hands under one side of it, the work went faster. With a mighty effort the boys heaved the stone all the way up, and it landed with a dull *clunk* on the chapel floor. Fergie shone his flashlight into the opening, and the boys saw a flight of worn stone steps leading down.

For quite a long while the boys knelt there, staring into the blackness. By now Masterman surely knew that they were there. What was he doing? Neither boy wanted to go down into that black hole, but somebody had to if Father Higgins was to be saved. Suddenly Johnny stood up. He put the chain of the crucifix around his neck and gripped his flashlight. "I'll go," he announced bravely, and he started down the steps. Fergie was so stunned that he just knelt there, openmouthed, and watched his friend plunge into the opening. Then he jumped up and cried, *"I'm with you, John baby!"* Setting his jaw grimly, Fergie started down the stairs after his friend.

A smell of mold and decay rose to the boys' nostrils, but they plodded on down the steep stairway. Cobwebs brushed their faces, but they waved them out of the way. Dampness clung to their bodies. The steps turned to the right and continued down, till Johnny and Fergie saw a doorway that was lit by a faint flickering glow. They walked on, with each step making them more frightened and more tense. At last they stood before the elaborately decorated arch. Monster heads and mysterious symbols were carved on it, and a grinning stone skull leered down from the top of the arch. With timid steps the boys shuffled closer, and when they stood at last in the doorway, they saw a fearful sight. A circular room lay before them, and around its walls ran one long stone bench. On the bench sat five mummies. Their eyes were empty holes, and their lipless mouths gaped. Each wore the tattered white costume of a monk. Some hoods were thrown back, while others were pulled close over withered, crumbling faces. But under the robes a tarnished glimmer showed that the mummies wore breastplates of steel, and each held a rusty sword in his right hand. In the center of the room stood a low stone table, and on it lay a burning candle and a half circle of green glass with a ragged, broken edge. Nearby stood the creature who called himself Rufus Masterman. The trembling, pale light hovered about his face. In his long bony hand he held another half circle of glass.

When he saw the boys, Masterman smiled scornfully. He glanced at the silver chain and crucifix that hung around Johnny's neck, and he laughed.

"Do you think that thing will protect you?" he snarled. "It would not prolong your life for a second, if I chose to kill you." And with that, Masterman stretched out his left hand. There was a snapping sound, and the crucifix broke from the chain and fell to the floor. Fear filled the hearts of the boys. What would happen to them now?

"You see?" Masterman said with an evil leer. "Holy trinkets are not much good against the knights who worship the Prince of the Air. He is the master of the still stars and flaming door, and tonight his faithful servants will rise from their long sleep. I will decide what to do with you two when I have finished my task. Maybe you will live in terrible insanity for the rest of your lives. Or maybe you will be buried alive here in this room, and turn to rotting skeletons. But all that will be decided presently. When I fit the two halves of the Great Circle together, I will undo the work of a pack of foul meddling fools. And the dead will live again."

Masterman closed his eyes and made a sign in the air. His face began to waver and shimmer, and the boys no longer saw the long, horsy face of the old clergyman. Instead they saw a hollow-eyed, haggard, cruel-looking man with long, dirty, yellow hair and a straggling blond beard. The man began to speak in Latin, and it was clear he was reciting a prayer or incantation of some sort. Stiff and still, the boys watched as he stepped forward with the piece of glass in his left hand. He bent to fit the two pieces together—but what was this? His hand shook and jerked back. Again he tried, and again the hand twitched away. With an angry roar, the man reached out with his other hand to stop the uncontrollable shaking of his left arm. He seemed calm again, but just as he was bending over the stone table again, he suddenly fell to his knees. As Johnny and Fergie watched in amazement, the man raised his arm and brought the piece of green glass smashing down hard on the stone table. The glass shattered into a thousand glittering pieces, and at that moment something incredible happened: With a dry, rustling sound the five mummies rose to their feet. They raised their rusty swords above their heads, and with a horrible unearthly screech they rushed at the figure who knelt by the table, a figure that now looked like Father Higgins! With a frantic lunge Father Higgins grabbed the other piece of glass and smashed it too. Instantly, the mummies collapsed to the floor.

CHAPTER TWELVE

For a long time Johnny and Fergie stood staring at the grim scene that lay before them. The mummies were crumpled on the floor near the table with swords still clutched in their clawlike hands. Bits of green glass were scattered all over the room, and Father Higgins stood in the middle of the floor, tottering and swaying. He was wearing his usual black clerical pants and jacket and stiff white Roman collar. His face was deathly pale, but he smiled when he saw the boys.

"Greetings, gentlemen!" he said. "You meet the strangest people in the strangest places, don't you?" And with that he began to cry and stretched out both arms to the boys, who rushed forward to hug him.

It was quite a while before the three of them could

pull themselves together. Father Higgins seemed a little woozy, but otherwise he acted like himself. After a short while he wiped his eyes clumsily with his sleeve and looked around at the corpses. "Where are we?" asked Father Higgins as he shook his head in wonderment.

"We're on a little island off the coast of England," answered Johnny. "The professor and the two of us followed you and . . ."

"The *professor*?" exclaimed Father Higgins. "Where is he?"

Johnny and Fergie looked at each other. They didn't know how to explain the awful thing that had happened in Ilfracombe, and they didn't feel like trying now.

"We'll tell you later, Father," said Johnny quietly. "Right now I think we all ought to get out of here."

The priest nodded and followed the boys to the archway. But as they were about to leave, the three of them turned. Something odd and wonderful was happening: Bits of dust were falling out of the air, like flakes of snow. This enchanted room had been spotless before, but now the dust of centuries was sifting down to cover the bodies of the evil knights. Father Higgins made the sign of the cross, and then he and the boys left the room and began climbing the worn stone steps.

When they reached the top and stepped onto the floor of the ruined chapel, Johnny and Fergie heaved a deep sigh of relief. They gulped the salty-smelling night air into their lungs and looked up at the starry sky. Directly overhead a bright star burned, and as he watched it, something stirred in Johnny's mind.

"Father?" he asked, pointing up. "What's that star?"

Father Higgins peered up. Astronomy was one of his hobbies, so it didn't take long for him to come up with an answer. "That would be Vega, I think," he said. "Yes . . . at this time of year that's what it would be. Why?"

Johnny smiled. Another piece of the puzzle had fallen into place. *When Vega is high in the sky,* said one of the mysterious notes. Masterman had to wait for Vega before he could do his dirty work. "Oh, no particular reason," murmured Johnny. "I was just curious."

There was an awkward silence, and then Fergie spoke up. "Father," he asked, "do you mean you don't remember anything about smashing that green glass?"

Father Higgins looked bewildered. "Do you mean that piece of stained glass that I found in the church in Rocks Village? Is that what all those little fragments of glass were doing down there? Tell me . . . did I do the right thing?"

Fergie grinned broadly and patted the priest on the shoulder. "You sure did, Father. You sure did. But tell us: What's the last thing you remember? Before you woke up down in that room, I mean."

Father Higgins thought for a bit. "I was getting ready to go to do an emergency baptism. A newly born child was dying in St. Margaret's hospital, and so . . ." Father Higgins's voice trailed away, and he reached into the left-hand pocket of his jacket. What he pulled out was a small plastic squirt bottle with a symbol stamped on it. The symbol looked like this:

"Holy water!" exclaimed Johnny. "I'll bet that helped to save you—from Masterman, I mean."

Father Higgins scratched his chin and looked even more puzzled than he had before. "Somebody is going to have to fill me in on a lot of things," he said as he gazed around at the ruined walls. "But I guess that can wait till later. Right now I am unbelievably tired, and I hope there's a hotel on this island. You folks are going to have to lead the way—I still feel like someone who is walking in his sleep."

With Father Higgins's help, the boys got the stone slab back in place over the opening. Then Johnny and Fergie led their friend across the island and down the path to the inn. The innkeeper would be surprised the next morning when he found that the boys had an extra guest in their room, but they would make up some story to explain why he was there. When they were all back upstairs safe and sound, Johnny offered Father Higgins his bed. But the priest wouldn't hear of it.

"No, gentlemen," he said, yawning sleepily. "I slept on rocks and roots in the jungles during the Second World

War, and that floor looks very inviting to me. Wake me about noon tomorrow, if you would be so kind." After another yawn Father Higgins threw himself down on the rough boards, and in a few seconds he was sound asleep.

The next morning at breakfast the boys introduced the innkeeper to their friend. They explained that he was their uncle, who had come out on the late ferry the night before. Since the inn was closed, Father Higgins had spent the night sitting on the rocks by the harbor, and then near dawn one of the boys had let him in. The little tale seemed reasonable enough, and the innkeeper accepted it. After they had eaten, the boys paid their bill and asked if they could make a phone call to the Admiral Hood Inn in Ilfracombe. The innkeeper was a generous sort, so he let them do it, and they were overjoyed to find that the professor and Humphrey were back, safe and sound. Johnny gave them the arrival time of the next ferry, and said that he and Fergie would be on it. He added—somewhat mysteriously—that they were bringing a friend.

The three travelers said good-bye to the innkeeper and thanked him for his hospitality. Then they made their way down to the pier to wait for the steamboat. The trip back to Ilfracombe was a quick one on a calm sea, and when the ship came gliding into the harbor, two figures could be seen on the dock, waving cheerfully: the professor and his brother Humphrey. They were both grinning from ear to ear, and tears were running down their cheeks. When Father Higgins and the boys strode down the gangplank, the professor rushed forward and gave them each a big hug and told them how wonderful it was to see them again. Then he introduced Humphrey to Father Higgins and led them all to Humphrey's car. Johnny and Fergie looked at each other. They both wanted to know what had happened to the professor and Humphrey when they were imprisoned by Masterman's sorcery. But it was pretty clear from the way the professor was behaving that they weren't going to find out much—not now, anyway.

As it turned out, the professor and Humphrey were still staying at the Admiral Hood Inn. They had whipped up some sort of tale to explain why they had disappeared for twenty-four hours, and they actually told the truth about the two boys: When he was miraculously returned to this world, the professor guessed that the boys had gone out to Lundy. So he told this to the hotel's owner, a short, irritable man named George Greedy, and the owner believed it. When the boys came back, it seemed to prove that no one had been lying.

Later that day, everyone sat down to a big lunch in the dining room of the hotel. After they ate and chatted for a while, the professor coughed loudly and lit one of his stinky Russian cigarettes. This meant that he had an announcement to make, and from the look on his face he wasn't happy about it.

"Tom," he said, turning to Father Higgins, "I've told you that you were possessed by an evil spirit, but there's something else you should know. I don't know how to tell you, but . . ."

Father Higgins gazed at the professor. "Yes? But what?"

"Uh . . . just this," said the professor uncomfortably. "You . . . you broke into a church in Glastonbury and you, well, you ripped up the floor and stole your mother's ashes."

Father Higgins stared in amazement. "I *what*?"

"You did it while you were possessed," put in Humphrey with a kind smile. "Don't you have any memory of it?"

Father Higgins sighed. "Mercifully, no. I suppose Masterman made me think I was going to raise my mother from the dead, although he really had something more sinister in mind. But I don't understand why I didn't go through with it and let him complete the magic circle. Maybe the holy water I had in my pocket really helped, but I seemed to be completely in his control. Was I?"

The professor smiled. "Not quite. You're a strong-willed, stubborn person, and some part of your mind still belonged to you even when Masterman was calling the shots. So at the last moment you figured out what he was doing and wrecked his nice little plan. If his spirit is still hovering somewhere, I'll bet he is *furious*!"

Johnny squirmed uncomfortably in his seat. "Professor?" he asked in a faltering voice. "You don't think Masterman could come back, do you?"

The professor frowned and pursed up his lips. "I honestly don't know," he said slowly. "His spirit was strong enough to hang around on earth for centuries and haunt that fragment of glass that Higgy found in his church. But now that the glass has been shattered, I am hoping that Masterman has returned to the outer darkness, which is where he belongs."

Father Higgins toyed with a bit of food on his plate, and then he frowned. "Rod," he asked suddenly, "what has happened to my mother's ashes?"

"That's a good story all by itself," said the professor. "It seems that Masterman was staying at another hotel here in Ilfracombe—I believe it's called the Royal Britannia. Well, this morning the owner of the hotel reported him to the police as a missing person. So his luggage is probably down at the police station. Eventually it'll be examined, and they'll find the urn with your mother's ashes in it. There must be some kind of inscription on the urn, so it'll be returned to St. John's church in Glastonbury. Besides, the police down here must have heard about your little grave-robbing stunt. It was reported in the English newspapers."

There was an awkward pause. Johnny nibbled at a piece of sausage.

"Professor?" he said hesitantly. "How did you and Humphrey get away from Masterman?"

The professor coughed. "Well, to begin with," he said slowly, "I gather from what you and Fergie told me that it looked as if the two of us were inside a pair of bottles.

To us it didn't seem that way at all. It was as if we were trudging along over an endless sandy desert. The hot sun was beating down on our heads, and we wanted to collapse, but we couldn't. After what seemed like a very long time, we were suddenly dumped down in the street in front of the Admiral Hood Inn. I imagine that happened at the very moment when Higgy smashed those two hunks of glass." He turned to Father Higgins and bowed politely. "My thanks to you, Tom," he said, with a grin. "I wouldn't have enjoyed being a desert rat forever and ever."

Humphrey asked his friends if they wanted to stay in England and travel for a while. But everyone agreed that some other time might be best—after the experience they had had, they were anxious to get back home as soon as possible. However, Humphrey insisted that they spend a night at his house in Bristol before traveling to London to catch a plane. Besides, he said, it would take a little time to make travel arrangements. In the end, Humphrey didn't have to do any arm twisting. Everyone was delighted with a day to rest before their journey, and the professor enjoyed having a little more time to chat with his long-lost brother. So they packed their bags, paid their bills, and climbed into Humphrey's Bentley and roared off down the winding back roads that led to Bristol.

That evening Humphrey took his friends to Harvey's, an expensive and very nice restaurant in the downtown part of Bristol. Then, after a twilight walk across the Clifton Bridge, everyone settled down in Humphrey's house for a long, quiet evening. The three men gathered before the fireplace in Humphrey's living room, sipped sherry, and smoked some of Humphrey's excellent cigars. Johnny and Fergie played pool and pinball until they were sleepy and then dragged themselves off to bed. Quiet descended on the house, and Johnny stretched out in the roomy bed he had slept in just a few days before. The sheets smelled faintly musty, and the electric fire with its flickering red light still seemed homey and reassuring. Johnny sighed contentedly and rolled over to face the wall. For some reason, however, he couldn't go to sleep. He was beginning to get tense again, and he could hear his heart beating fast. He stared at the wavering red light that hovered on the wall. *Creak, creak.* Someone was walking along the hall outside his room. Surely it was Humphrey or one of the other two men. But then why did Johnny feel panic rising inside him? The creaking sounds died away, and then they came back. They halted outside Johnny's door. A knocking sound began . . . faintly. Johnny thought of his silver crucifix, but suddenly he realized that it was lying on the floor of the stone chamber where the De Marisco knights were entombed.

Knock, knock. Johnny forced himself to sit up and swing his legs out of bed. Probably his fears were foolish—he was having after-effects of the hideous experience he had gone through out on Lundy. Quickly Johnny got up and padded barefoot to the door. Gripping the large bronze knob, he pulled the door inward. There in the lighted hallway stood the ghostly figure of Masterman. He was bodiless now, and his shape shimmered and hovered in the air. But his lips were curled into an inhuman grin, and his eyes burned with the feverish glow of madness.

CHAPTER THIRTEEN

Johnny stood dead still, watching the evil, nightmarish face of the creature who stood before him. His lower jaw trembled and he wanted to scream, but he found that he couldn't. He wanted to close his eyes and faint, but he couldn't do that either. Masterman's lips did not move, but Johnny heard an angry, sneering voice that echoed inside his brain:

"Good evening, young man! Are you prepared to receive visitors? No? Then you must come out and join me. You may not enjoy the darkness I am sending you to, where every hour will seem like a year of sleepless pain, but my poor fellow knights must be avenged somehow. Come along. I will not take no for an answer!"

With that, Masterman motioned for Johnny to step forward, and Johnny found that he had to obey. Stumbling stiffly out into the hall like a robot, he began to follow the beckoning, eerie shape.

Suddenly a door slammed. Father Higgins stood in the hall, glowering angrily, the holy-water bottle in his hand. With a quick twist he unscrewed the cap and flung the liquid into Masterman's face. An inhuman howl arose as the creature writhed and twisted. His face turned to a melting horror and his body sagged and ran like water. In a few seconds there was nothing there at all except a faint scorch mark on the hall rug.

Johnny rushed to Father Higgins and threw his arms around him. Humphrey and Fergie and Professor Childermass came rushing into the hall in their pajamas. They looked frightened and wild-eyed.

"What in the name of heaven is going on?" raved the professor as he stuck his glasses crookedly onto his nose. Johnny turned his tear-streaked face toward the professor, and in a flash the old man guessed. "Masterman!" he roared. "He's come back!"

Father Higgins nodded solemnly. "At least he isn't using my body this time," he growled. "But poor John here almost got dragged away to . . . to God knows where." Father Higgins turned to Humphrey. "See here now!" he said. "Roderick tells me that you know something about magic. Can you figure out how that fiend managed to return?"

Humphrey shook his head. "Offhand, I couldn't say,"

he replied. "Unless . . . unless . . ." Suddenly he turned to Johnny. "Would you let me examine the clothes you were wearing the day you were in the underground room?" he asked excitedly.

Johnny was startled, and he couldn't imagine what Humphrey was driving at. But he led him into his room. Except for underwear and socks, the clothes he had been wearing at bedtime were the ones he had worn in the tomb chamber: a red plaid shirt and brown corduroy pants. They lay draped over the chair next to the bed. Carefully Humphrey examined the shirt. He peered into the pocket and put his hand inside the cuffs. Sighing, he put the shirt aside and went to work on the pants. Meanwhile, Father Higgins, Fergie, and the professor crowded into the room and stood watching curiously.

"What in blazes do you expect to find?" snapped the professor.

"Just be patient, brother," muttered Humphrey as he began running his forefinger inside one of Johnny's pant cuffs. "If I'm right, then . . . Hah!" With that, Humphrey reached into the cuff and pulled something out. He turned to the others with his palm open before him. On it lay a tiny golden fish.

"One of those!" gasped the professor. "I don't believe it! It must have landed in Johnny's cuff when Higgy broke one of the pieces of glass!"

Humphrey nodded. "I expect that that is what happened. I remember now that you told me the piece of glass Father Higgins found had little golden fish embedded in it," he said.

"What do we do with it?" asked Johnny. He was afraid that this would turn out to be one of those awful cursed objects that couldn't be gotten rid of.

Humphrey smiled in a secretive way. "Let us all go downstairs to my basement laboratory while I unmagic this widget."

Since he dabbled in alchemy and sorcery, Humphrey had a basement workshop that looked as if it belonged to a mad scientist. Bubbling retorts, racks of test tubes, spiraling glass tubes, and liquids of various colors dripping into beakers were everywhere. And on one marble-topped table was a small metal smelting furnace. The fire inside had been banked, but it was not out, and as the others stood watching, Humphrey used a pair of bellows to get the coals glowing. When the fire was going again, Humphrey picked up a pair of tweezers and used it to drop the tiny fish into the hole in the top of the furnace. Then he put the iron lid on the hole and stood humming quietly. Gold melts at a fairly low temperature, so he didn't have long to wait. Finally he opened up the furnace again and peeked inside.

"Ah!" he said. "Perfect!" And he reached in carefully with a long-handled pair of tongs to pull out a shapeless blob of yellow metal. Smiling, Humphrey laid the blob on the marble to let it cool.

"There!" he said. "If you change an amulet's shape,

the magic force runs out of it—at least that is what the great experts say. To be doubly sure, we'll take this thing down to the bridge, put it in a matchbox, and pitch it into the river."

"I hope this really will be the end," sighed the professor. "My heart isn't quite as strong as it used to be."

"Neither is mine," added Johnny, shuddering slightly.

The professor, Father Higgins, and the two boys were a bit sad about leaving friendly old Humphrey and his marvelous eccentric home. But they really were anxious to get back to Duston Heights, so the next day they made travel arrangements. The professor reserved four seats on a flight leaving London at four P.M. the following day. At first everyone worried about Father Higgins's passport, but it was found securely buttoned into an inner pocket of his clerical jacket. Apparently Masterman had made Father Higgins look like Father Higgins again in order to get past the passport officials.

Sadly on the following morning, the travelers said good-bye to Humphrey on the platform of Bristol Temple Meads railway station. The trip to London was fast, and from Paddington station they took a cab to the airport for the long journey home. The professor's car was waiting for him at the Boston airport, and they all threw themselves and their luggage wearily into the old maroon Pontiac for the final ride home. It was about dawn when they rolled into Duston Heights, and though he was sleepy, Johnny thought he had never seen any town that looked so beautiful. It was too late to wake up the Dixons or the Fergusons, so Johnny and Fergie stayed what remained of the night at the professor's house. Father Higgins stayed too, because he was exhausted and didn't want the professor to drive him to Rocks Village that night.

A week passed, and Johnny got little pieces of information. Father Higgins returned to his parish, and hardly anyone accepted the story that he had suffered an attack of amnesia brought on by the flare-up of an old head wound he had gotten during World War Two. The professor saw a small item in the London *Times* that said that the ashes of Mrs. Mary Higgins had been recovered and reburied under the floor of St. John's church in Glastonbury. Another item in the same paper said that the disappearance of Dr. Rufus Masterman from his hotel room in Ilfracombe remained unsolved, but the police were still making inquiries. Finally, at the end of the summer, the best news of all arrived: Father Higgins was going to be transferred back to his old parish of St. Michael's in Duston Heights. The bishop had received a lot of complaint letters from members of the Rocks Village parish. When Father Higgins had disappeared and then returned claiming amnesia, many people felt that it proved he was totally out of his mind. So back he went to St. Michael's. Needless to say, the Dixons were overjoyed to get their old pastor back, and of course Johnny, Fergie, and the professor were happy too. So at last things seemed to be getting back to normal.

When Father Higgins returned to St. Michael's after Labor Day, the professor threw a backyard barbecue to celebrate. He cooked hamburgers and hot dogs on the backyard grill, and laid in a big supply of lemonade, iced tea, and soft drinks. Chinese lanterns were rigged up on clotheslines that were strung through the trees in the yard, and of course the professor wore his tasteless apron with witty sayings and his puffy white chef's hat. The professor's good friend Dr. Charles Coote came down from Durham, New Hampshire, for the fest. He was a tall, gawky man with a bumpy ridged nose and big goggly glasses who taught at the University of New Hampshire, and he knew a lot about magic and the occult. Johnny's grandparents came to the party too.

Everyone had a glorious time. The boys wolfed hot dogs and hamburgers, and Grampa Dixon beat the professor at horseshoes. Fergie then beat both of them. The Dixons went home early as usual, and the others inspected the bedraggled, weedy wreckage of the professor's flower garden. He never had the time or energy to get it in shape, and it looked thoroughly dreadful. It was a lovely cool evening, and a gentle breeze rocked the Chinese lanterns. Fireflies winked among the tall weeds, and a few crickets could still be heard in the grass. For a long time no one said anything. Father

Higgins swirled the brandy in his glass and looked thoughtful. Finally he spoke up.

"Dr. Coote," he asked slowly, "why do you think Masterman picked on me? Is it because I'm superstitious and believe in ghosts?"

Dr. Coote laughed. "My dear Father Higgins," he said, "I don't think your beliefs had anything to do with what happened to you. To tell you the truth, you just were *susceptible.* You really wanted to talk to your dead mother and iron things out, and the spirit of Masterman used that to his own advantage. Remember one of the notes that you found in your house? *You may be wrong about everything.* Some kindly power was trying to warn you."

Father Higgins made grumbly noises and sipped his brandy. "All right then," he said, poking a hairy finger at Dr. Coote. "Answer this one for me: How did that dratted hunk of glass get into my church? Who put it there?"

Dr. Coote scratched his head. "Hard to say. Your church is over two hundred years old, and I've heard stories that there was a very rich man who lived in Rocks Village in the late 1700's who made trips to Europe and brought back ancient objects. He probably discovered that the glass fragment had evil powers. Maybe he put it in the church to hold its evil in check. One thing I can say for sure: Masterman never put the glass in the church. He was a disembodied ghost who haunted the glass, and he couldn't have turned a doorknob with his shadowy hands. That was why he needed your help, Father. He needed a real human body with real hands, so that he could shove those two pieces of glass together and complete the circle."

Fergie was standing nearby, sipping soda pop. "Hey, Dr. Coote," he said suddenly, "what do you think those creepy knights would've done if they had gotten loose?"

Dr. Coote frowned. "I hate to think what those wretches would have done," he said, staring off at the night sky. "I've heard tales of men who could turn themselves into superhuman beings by doing unspeakable things—like eating the hearts of other humans. Would you like it if someone could get inside your head and listen in on your thoughts? Or make you imagine that you were somebody else? Let's just say that those knights could have made life very difficult for a lot of people—maybe for everybody on earth."

It was getting late, and everyone was feeling tired. The professor yawned, flapping his hand in front of his mouth. It was contagious. Father Higgins yawned, and so did Dr. Coote. Soon everyone was walking slowly back toward the lighted house. Johnny felt exhausted, but he still had one more question rattling around in his head.

"Uh, professor?" he asked timidly. "Is your brother really a sorcerer? I mean, he saved us out on the bridge, but then he got trapped by Masterman just the way you did."

The professor chuckled. "Humphrey would like to

think he's a sorcerer," he said. "He's memorized some spells and he's whipped up some potions in his lab, but that doesn't make you a wizard. Just before we left, he told me he was going to stop fooling around with magic."

"Do you think he really will?" asked Johnny.

The professor grinned and peered at Johnny over the top of his glasses. "John," he said solemnly, "if I told you I was going to stop being a foul-tempered old crank, what would you believe? Eh?"

Everybody laughed.

JOHN BELLAIRS

is the critically acclaimed, best-selling author of many Gothic novels, including *The House with a Clock in Its Walls* trilogy, *The Dark Secret of Weatherend*, *The Lamp from the Warlock's Tomb*, and the previous novels starring Johnny Dixon and Professor Childermass: *The Curse of the Blue Figurine; The Mummy, the Will, and the Crypt; The Spell of the Sorcerer's Skull; The Revenge of the Wizard's Ghost; The Eyes of the Killer Robot*; and *The Chessmen of Doom*.

A resident of Haverhill, Massachusetts, Mr. Bellairs is currently at work on another chilling tale.